Night Visitors © 2017 Owen Keehnen

Published by Out Tales Publishing

978-0-9992172-3-8
Cover Art by Adrian Nicholas

Night Visitors

By Owen Keehnen

For my husband, Carl.

To suspect your own mortality is to know the beginning of terror, to learn irrefutably that you are mortal is to know the end of terror.

- Frank Herbert

IN THE DARK

When we first arrived at the hospital I ran screaming to the front desk. Simon was still in the car. Still breathing, but I didn't think he would live through the night. He was so pale, so weak, so seemingly drained of life. His lips and nail beds were white. His protruding tongue was chalky. Even his skin was cool to the touch. On the drive to the emergency room Simon kept drifting in and out of consciousness and repeating "I'm fine. It's nothing." He was in shock from the attack. He'd seen the hideous things that had sunk their teeth into the flesh. I'd wrapped the wound as best I could, but a good amount of meat had been torn from his bones.

Last night when I heard his anguished cry from the tent, my blood ran cold. The hairs at the nape of my neck stirred with a primal knowing. Only a being in agony was capable of producing that sound. I searched the tent for a weapon. We hadn't brought anything like that along. Everyone said camping was safe these days. "Really safe, unless you're stupid." They were wrong. I'm not stupid and camping isn't safe. Not always. Not everywhere. Nothing is.

A moment later, Simon's initial cry was followed by a longer wail. I stepped into the night. Stars. Darkness. The gibbous moon emerged from behind a cloud, bathing the landscape in a golden glow, transforming this patch of wilderness into an alien terrain. He was in the distance, grunting with exertion. Panic. Pain. Simon was crawling towards the tent, gritting his teeth as he pulled himself with his arms. I ran to him and tried to pull him along. He fought me at first, wild eyed and flailing, no doubt fearing his attacker had returned. Eventually he recognized me and stopped struggling. I pulled him back inside the tent and zipped the entrance closed. Not much protection, but something. I handed Simon the whiskey. He took a long drink. Then another. He still had not uttered a word.

Once he seemed able to respond I spoke low and asked, "What happened?" I didn't want whatever was out there to hear.

The liquor calmed him, but he was still trembling, still unable to speak. I saw in his eyes that his mind was still caught in the moment of the mauling. At first, I tried to refrain from inspecting his injury, but I needed to overcome my squeamishness and take action. I knew it was bad. I'd seen the blood on his shredded jeans. The dark glisten of a stain spreading, like the bloom of a flower or a plume of smoke.

I used my pocketknife to remove what remained of the lower leg of his pants. Sopping red. On his shin were four puncture wounds. A trickle of blood surrounded each hole. The real carnage was higher, in the region which had once housed his calf. The flesh had been ripped away. Only bits of muscle and sinew still clung to the bone. Gristle. In places denim blended with gnarled flesh into a pulpy mass. I closed my eyes to hold off my nausea. When it passed I opened them again. The wound needed to be cleaned. I took the whiskey bottle from Simon's hand and took a swig. I warned him this would hurt. He grabbed my other hand as I poured the alcohol over the area. He thrashed in agony. Teeth gritted. Hair limp with sweat. His grip nearly broke my hand. The sting of sterilization roused him.

He sat up. Handsome face still contorted from pain.

I asked him again what happened.

"That thing, it was…"

I offered another guzzle of whiskey.

He took a long drink and winced from either the wound or the whiskey. "… Crouched behind a pile of wood."

"What was?" Crouched was an odd term for an animal.

"Dead."

The single word chilled me. I had no idea what he meant. That made it worse. As he took another swig, I rummaged through my backpack. A flannel shirt would serve as a makeshift tourniquet. I tore it into strips and used a length of fabric to wrap around the area above his knee. More strips lower. Tighter around the bitten area. Maybe that would isolate the wound. Minimize blood loss. The task was a distraction from Simon's mumbling.

"Dead and yet watching me. Waiting."

I attributed his distressed babble to shock. He was already so pale. So drained. He needed medical attention. I had to get him to a hospital as soon as possible. The car was parked a few hundred feet up the path. Simon easily outweighed me by seventy pounds. Too big to carry. I doubted I could even support his weight.

Grabbing a knife and flashlight, I ran outside. The full moon had moved behind a dark expanse of clouds. I scanned the area, looking for an appropriate walking stick for Simon. I passed the flashlight beam along the ground and through the woods. Nothing. As the light moved through the trees again, I saw them. Just ahead. Just beyond the circle of light. Perhaps a dozen jaundiced eyes watching, betraying grim creatures ahead or behind the light. Things that lurked in the shadows. At first I thought it was my eyes or a trick of the light. A ghost of illumination. Strange reflections. I moved the beam slower. There was no mistaking them. One set of eyes. Then more. Yellow as the weeping of an infected wound. A glowing mucous. Alert. Poised. Ready and yet unable. More eyes. When I moved the beam I noticed that the eyes, which had been in the darkness, were now closer. Some had begun to spread and circle to either side. I ran back in the tent and zipped the flap. I checked the fuel on the lantern. Thankfully it was full. More than enough to last until morning. If we lasted until morning.

Simon asked what was happening.

My behavior said everything. "Eyes."

"Eyes." When he repeated the word a strange transformation occurred. Rather than sparking panic, Simon's mood seemed to lighten. His bemused look made no sense, given the circumstances. "Eyes," he once again. At the time I attributed it all to delirium and residual shock.

I heard the creatures outside. Rustling and then... sniffing. More than one. Beasts. I saw their twisted upright silhouettes moving in shadows across the blue nylon walls. Pacing. Snarling. Eager to gain entry. I wondered why they hesitated. The fabric seemed no match for claws and teeth, Yet, the tent wall kept them at bay, at least for now. Maybe it was the lantern light they feared. I took a couple pictures with my phone. If the light had frightened or pained them, maybe the flash would drive them further away. But the flash had little added impact. The creatures remained in the shadows outside the tent.

I cradled Simon as he floated in and out of consciousness. I knew the creatures only as shadows and eyes. I still had not seen them. I was unsure if they were animal or human. No telling from the shadows or the snarls. My unmoored imagination ran rampant. Maybe

11

those silhouettes were cast by a hideous combination of man and beast. The yellow eyes were feral. Menacing. Capable of malevolence. Starved. The eyes displayed an intelligence and yet they also seemed beyond reason. Raw hatred. Pure hunger. Those eyes saw me as food, meat, sustenance. I was inconsequential, apart from my flesh. The scent of primal terror probably whet their hunger all the more.

I must have slept because the next thing I knew, dawn was breaking. I sat up quickly, shaken but alert. I wondered if it was all a dream, and those creatures were no more than phantoms of the night. Simon took a jagged breath. I turned to see him fevered and pale beside me. My nightmare was real... and not yet over.

Simon needed a doctor. I unzipped the tent. As the metal teeth parted, the clearing emerged. The sun was brightening the tree line. Birds were clamorous. I unzipped the tent door a bit more and stuck my head out the opening. The morning chill hit me. My breath was a fog. There was no one, no things, about. In the dirt encircling the tent were footprints. Shoes? Were those creatures human? I wondered if the prints could have been Simon's or mine, but they were of varying sizes. There wasn't time to wonder. This was the time for action.

I told Simon I was going to find something to help him walk.

He attempted to move, but fell back in pain.

There was a branch near the edge of the clearing. Picking up the stick, I stood motionless and waited for the slightest hint of the intruders' return. Nothing usual. Birds. Squirrels. Last night seemed utterly fantastic in the light of day. But there was no denying the attack, or Simon's injury. Maybe it was the rest that I'd imagined.

The shadows. The eyes. All I knew for certain was that those things were gone... for now.

I left our tent and gear. I slung our backpacks over either arm and took nothing more. Simon leaned on me and used the walking stick as support. The trek down the uneven path was slow going. Eventually we made it to the car. When the engine roared to life I realized I'd been holding my breath. We'd passed a hospital in one of the nearby Michigan towns, but I couldn't recall which one. After a few hours on secondary roads, all those quaint villages blend together. I didn't remember it as being too far.

The hospital was twenty minutes away.

By the time we arrived at the emergency entrance, Simon looked like death. Sweaty. White with reddish rings beneath his eyes. He was clammy. Cold. As the door whooshed open we fell into the coolness and that familiar sterile smell. I cried for help. My voice sounded unusually loud. They took him immediately.

The nurse watched me fill out the paperwork. "You're a stranger in town, aren't you?"

I nodded.

"Thought so."

I was never a great conversationalist. At present I had no capacity for small talk.

The doctor emerged a moment later. He flipped through the paperwork I'd filled out and asked if I'd seen what happened. I said I only witnessed the aftermath, but said I might have a picture of what had attacked Simon on my phone. The doctor looked up from the forms. He said he'd like to see. I flipped to my photo file. The flash had obliterated the shadows, but in the same pictures the flash caused Simon's eyes to turn a familiar, ocher shade. I thought I'd taken more pictures. Only two were currently available. I said that sometimes, when reception was poor, pictures get sent directly to the cloud and show up on my phone later.

"Amazing how that all works."

I agreed.

"Not to worry." The doctor gave instructions to administer antibiotics. He added that he had a good idea of what we were dealing with.

I asked him what.

He said he could say just yet.

When I suggested giving Simon a rabies test and a tetanus shot, the doctor said that wouldn't be necessary. His tone made it clear he thought I was an oaf. Smug bastard. His beeper sounded and he was down the hall and away.

The medics gave Simon a blood transfusion. They were drawing vial after vial of blood for testing. I'd never seen so much blood for tests. As though they were draining him. At one point I worried that collecting so much blood would kill him. I buzzed the nurse and asked if anyone was keeping track of how much they were taking.

She was about to say something when Dr. Smug returned. He knew what we were discussing. He said they were flushing his system. "He'll be a new man by morning." Another transfusion. Though skeptical, the draining and insurgence of blood did seem to give have a positive impact. Simon's coloring was better. I apologized. The stress of everything had made me irritable. Best leave this to the experts.

The doctor said not to worry and asked more questions about what I'd seen at the campsite. Maybe he was trying to prove he had a bedside manner. Finally I turned back to Simon, "Shouldn't you tend to him? The transfusions and antibiotics seem to be helping, but what about that wound on his leg." Dr. Smug turned back to Simon.

Eventually they administered painkillers. By then he'd been transferred to an actual room. Dusk returned. Outside, the silhouettes of barren trees stood stark against the purpled underbellies of clouds along the horizon. This was the light that ushered in the darkness.

I sat at his bedside and stared at my phone. I should be calling someone, but I had no idea whom. We'd been dating less than a month. We met online and hooked up a few times since. The sex was incredible. Wild. Unpredictable. Exciting. Always leaving me wanting more. Simon already had this trip planned. He camped in the area every year. "It's in my blood," he'd said. When he asked if I'd like to get away for the weekend, I jumped at the chance. I'd sooner spend time with him in a luxury hotel, but I was willing to rough it. This was the first time we'd spent a significant amount of time together outside the bedroom.

Sitting there I realized how little I knew about Simon. I'd never met his friends or seen pictures of his family. He never mentioned a relative or a pal or anyone special that I could recall. I figured he was a lot like me, mostly alone in the big city and the world. Maybe I'd been projecting. I wasn't even sure where he was from. The area? Was that why he came here every year? I'd already checked his wallet. Nothing more than his name and current address. His last name was Johnson.

Last week I was feeling a little dreamy after one of our trysts and tried to stalk him online. Simon Johnson had no Internet presence I could find. No Facebook. No LinkedIn. No Instagram. At the time I thought it cute he wasn't on social media. I wasn't even sure where he

15

worked or what he did, something in sales and finance. Insurance? Investments?

Despite the tranquilizers, Simon was restless. He kicked and pulled at the blanket. During one of his anxious fits, I saw something. At first, I was sure it was a shadow or a trick of the blanket's fold. I bent closer and eventually reached out to touch. I hadn't been imagining things. His foot was gone. There was only an indentation on the sheet where it had been. His foot was no longer attached. I pushed the blanket aside. His lower left leg was also missing. Had there been a procedure I knew nothing about? I'd been in the room the entire time except for a bathroom break or two.

I flipped on the bedside lamp. As my eyes adjusted, the hallucination vanished. Simon's foot was discolored below the thick bandages about his calf, but it was still there, still very much attached. I attributed what I had seen, or imagined, to exhaustion and hunger. But I'd felt the space. The absence. Could hallucinations be tactile, as well? It was upsetting, but I was grateful I'd been mistaken. I rearranged his blankets. The light clicked off of its own accord. Evidently it was on some sort of timer.

In a moment, Simon's restless kicking resumed. Fevered. Disturbed. He scratched himself and shifted and even sported an erection. I tried to straighten the sheet and blankets, but everything had shifted again. Once more there was an absence where his foot should have been. Hallucinations, like lightning, rarely strike twice in the same spot... but there are exceptions. I bent closer. Touched the emptiness. The absence had spread to his upper thigh. No flesh. No bone. No blood. Nothing. The sheet wasn't even warm. The disappearance was spreading and the vanishing seemed to put Simon in a state of great ecstasy rather than pain. His moans grew.

I should have stayed and pressed the call button. As much as I needed someone to validate what I was seeing, I also had to escape that room and whatever was happening to him. I ran into the hallway. "There's something wrong," I shouted towards the nurse's station.

Two people behind the desk rose. One began running and met me outside the door. He wore a smile instead of a look of concern. His focus was on me instead of what was happening inside the room. I pointed to the bed. "Something's wrong. He's changed."

The orderly flipped on the light at the door and entered.

Simon appeared to be sleeping soundly. His formerly absent leg was exposed. The orderly exchanged a look with the nurse at the door. I knew what they were thinking. They assumed I was exhausted and distraught and had hallucinated the entire thing. I wondered the same thing myself. But it happened twice. I touched the spot where his foot should've been. Twice.

"He seems fine now. Just resting." The orderly offered a smile. "You're a stranger in town, aren't you?"

Why was everyone asking that? What did it have to do with anything?   The nurse put a hand on my forearm. "Why don't you get out of here and get some rest? There's nothing more to be done here tonight." She was being thoughtful. She was right. Clearly, I was on edge. I needed sleep or to leave for a bit and clear my head. I asked about lodgings nearby. She mentioned a motel a half mile down the road. "Real nice rooms." She scribbled the name of the place and directions. I left my cell phone number and said if there were any changes in his condition to give me a call.

Once outside, I realized how stale the hospital air had been. I drove towards the highway with the windows down. The cool night air felt wonderful. I fiddled with the radio. No reception. I was tempted to keep driving for a bit, but then I saw the neon vacancy sign at the motel the nurse had mentioned. Just a twelve-unit, one-story string of rooms off the highway. Nothing fancy. Just a place to lay my head.

Only one other car was in the lot. I suspected it belonged to the old codger smoking a Kool at the front desk. He eyed me suspiciously as soon as I came through the door. I was readied for him to ask if I was a stranger in town. Instead, he said nothing. Maybe he didn't need to ask. The television was loud. Wheel of Fortune. He finally spoke to quote the cost of a room. "$39 a night." I handed over my credit card and a minute later he handed me the key to Room 103 and the menu to a pizza place. "They deliver all night," he added.

"Thanks. I'm more tired than hungry."

"Suit yourself, just a suggestion." He was getting downright chatty. He never rose from his chair on wheels

I moved the car closer to the room, grabbed my bag from the backseat, and opened the door to Room 103. Musty. This place hadn't been aired out in a while. With some effort I cracked the window. Other than the stale air, everything about the room was $39 worth of fine. I wasn't staying here longer than necessary, only until Simon was well enough to be moved. I stretched out on the bed. Fatigue pressed down like a weight. I was even more exhausted than I thought. I was asleep in two minutes. Didn't even bother to brush my teeth or take off my shoes.

When the phone rang at a little after 1:00 AM I was still sound asleep. I looked at my cell. Unknown number. I figured it was the hospital. After a pause the woman on the phone asked if Simon was with me.

All lingering fuzziness of sleep fell away. "What?"

"Has Mr. Johnson joined you at the motel?"

I sat up in bed. "Isn't he there?"

Another pause, longer. "Unfortunately, your friend has gone temporarily missing."

"What? I don't understand."

Apparently when the nurse made her midnight rounds, she found Simon's bed empty. "The sheets weren't even warm," the nurse added. I suspected that was more information than she was supposed to divulge.

"So, he's been gone a while?"

"That's what we're trying to find out."

The disturbing absence of his foot and leg came immediately to mind. I almost said something, but was unsure how to explain it. The nurse would only think me mad. I said that to my knowledge Simon was too ill to leave, especially on his own. Another long pause. The nurse said that, according to her report, he was doing fine. That's why she called to be sure he hadn't left with me.

"Even with his leg injury?"

She paused. I heard the flipping of sheets and pages. She said she wasn't aware of that. "There is no record in the report... nothing to suggest a lack of mobility."

What kind of hospital was this? I assumed she was not the nurse watching him, but simply the person delegated with calling. I let the comment slide and simply said I was alone. I heard someone whispering to her in the background. Hushed. Coaching, perhaps. The nurse replied to the unheard comment before returning to the line. Her tone had changed. She tried to sound confident and said, "We'll search the area again. No need for concern. I'm sure he'll turn up."

When I last saw Simon, he unconscious and fevered. A report that he was fine had to be mistaken. As far as I was concerned, the only explanation for his absence was that he had been taken. Or perhaps his condition had improved drastically. The doctor said it would. Could he possibly improve enough to leave the hospital of his own volition in the middle of the night? Maybe he had vanished in a different way. Maybe the disappearing I'd witnessed had continued. The moment the thought occurred to me, I discounted it as absurd. My imagination was running wild. I suspected the real reason for his disappearance was something mundane. Probably a hospital mix-up. Maybe he'd been taken for a test and the attending nursing staff hadn't been informed. Lack of communication between physicians and staff and various medical departments was commonplace in hospitals. Maybe someone had just written down the wrong room number.

I noticed my phone battery was at less than 20%. This would be a terrible time to run out. I was almost sure my charger was in the car. Hopefully I hadn't brought it into the hospital and left it, or worse, left it at the campsite. I grabbed my car keys. Though the moon was mostly obscured, the stars were plentiful. Simon had described it as "a brilliant canopy." He was right. This was not a typical urban sight.

The stars were what had sparked this camping trip. Simon already had the trip planned. He asked me to come along. He wanted me to see the stars outside of the city lights. "They'll leave you in awe," he'd said. Simon was a seasoned camper. He said we could make it a romantic getaway. That was all he needed to say. By then I was already smitten by him. He pulled me close and kissed me in a way that could convince me of anything. "I'd love to go with you," I said a moment later. Though it was just last week, the memory seemed distant. That moment was a universe removed from this town and this lonely motel lot.

The car was a couple of spaces over. My footsteps sounded unnaturally loud on the asphalt. The past 24 hours had been upsetting, to say the least. I caught myself holding my breath. Relax, I thought, bending and opening the car door. Relax. Simon's dried blood was on the passenger seat. Relax. Thank God the charger was plugged into the cigarette lighter.

I sensed something even before I heard the crackling. It came from the dense woods at the edge of the lot. The light wind at my back carried a whisper of menace. The hair stood on my arms and at the back of my neck. Someone or something was moving through the wooded underbrush. I stilled myself, hoping this was another folly of my imagination. The crackling of slow movement resumed. Whatever was out there was trying not to be heard. The sound blended at times with the wind, the hum of highway traffic, and the canned laughter from the motel office TV. This was real. Something was out there. Watching. Waiting in the woods. I was sure of it. I stared into the darkness until I could see the trees and grasses and underbrush. In my peripheral vision, I saw the shaking of a branch. When the moon slipped behind a cloud, the yellow eyes appeared. Eyes similar to those I'd seen last night. The eyes of Simon's savage attackers. I eased the car door shut. No sudden movement. Not yet. I readied my key and dashed to Room 103, fumbling with the lock. Had the eyes come nearer? Were they moving across the lot? Was that breath at my neck or the breeze? I was too terrified to look. I bolted and flipped the sliding latch on the door and slammed the cracked motel window. Fresh air was not something I was willing to die for and I knew whatever lurked out there wanted to kill me.

Shaking, I phoned the police. The line connected immediately. My words were a panicked jumble. I said I'd seen something suspicious in the woods by the motel.

"What did you see?"

How could I explain? "I saw something in the trees beyond the parking lot. I think it might have been the same thing that attacked my friend last night at the campsite outside of town."

There was a pause and flipping of papers. "We show no record of an attack last night."

"Well, I don't know if it was officially reported or not, but it happened. My friend is at the hospital." I almost added, "At least he was," but assumed that would complicate matters. Instead I said, "The thing that attacked him is here, in the woods. Maybe it thinks I saw something or know something. I feel like it's going to come for me."

"Thing. Animal? Person?"

I said I wasn't sure. "I know it has yellow eyes."

"Size?"

"Of the eyes?"

"Of this... creature."

I didn't know.

"Two legged? Four legged?"

I remembered the creatures circling the tent. Not paw prints, but footprints, not barefoot, wearing shoes. I found it hard to be sure of anything and even if I was certain, how could I explain it without sounding

22

certifiable. I hadn't really seen anything – only eyes, and footprints, and what was done to Simon. "I'm not quite sure what it is. Maybe part man and part beast. And there's more than one. I only saw one of them tonight." As soon as I finished speaking I was sure the dispatcher would hang up. To his credit, he didn't miss a beat. For lack of a better word he suggested predator.

I didn't care what they called them.

"So there is more than one?"

"Now? Probably. I don't know. Just send someone."

The dispatcher asked my name and Simon's name and the phone number. He had too many questions that he asked too slowly. He wanted too many inconsequential details. None of it seemed to matter right now.

"This is urgent. Something is out there. I can't tell you anything more. I need you to send someone."

He told me to remain inside. "Keep calm."

Did I sound hysterical? I realized I'd been shouting. He said a patrol car was coming to investigate.

"When."

Soon.

I watched and waited for what seemed an eternity. Ten minutes later, the squad car arrived. As it cruised the lot, the headlights panned across Room 103. The presence of the police alleviated some of my fear. Hopefully whatever prowled in those woods would flee at the sight. The patrol car cruised the lot with a searchlight before stopping on the edge of the asphalt, near where I'd seen the eyes.

I expected the officer to question me. Did they take my room number? Maybe the questions would come after he had searched. I heard the car door slam and saw

23

the stocky officer. Formidable. But alone. I could see his holster, handcuffs, and club. He crossed the tall grass and underbrush border of the woods. His flashlight beam slashed the darkness and bounced off the trunks of the oaks and birch. Moving deeper until only the ghost of the flashlight beam was visible. The light faded, weakening like the pulse of the dying.

I waited. For what? Nothing. A scream. The clap of a gunshot. Focused on the darkness where the officer had disappeared, I jumped at the ring of the motel phone. A nurse. Simon had been located. There'd been a miscommunication. He was in radiology. I figured it was a communication snafu. As I hung up I realized that when the hospital phoned earlier, it had been on my cell phone.

When I pulled back the curtain of Room 103, the squad car was gone.

I assumed the officer had found nothing. I expected him to check on me or at least give me the search results in person. To reassure me. To let me know he hadn't seen a thing and that evidently the "predator" had moved on. The lack of follow up was unusual. Maybe they just did things differently here.

Fifteen minutes later my cell phone rang. The police were calling to report they'd sent a squad car. I said I'd seen the officer searching the woods. "He's gone now."

The dispatcher asked if I'd spoken directly with the officer. I said no, when he arrived he went directly to where I'd seen the predator. "Then he went into the woods." I said when I didn't see him later, I assumed he'd found nothing and left. "He didn't find anything, did he?"

"So you didn't actually see him leave."

I said I'd been distracted by a phone call. Sensing the dispatcher's disapproval, I felt a need to explain. "The hospital was calling to say my friend had been found."

"Simon?"

"Yes." Had I told the officer his name? Probably. I'd been asked quite a few questions. My mind was cloudy with fatigue and the string of stressful events. Maybe the cops had followed up on my claims of an earlier attack at the campsite by calling the hospital.

The dispatcher asked again if I was sure I hadn't spoken with the officer.

"Of course I'm sure."

They hadn't heard from the officer. "Most unusual."

I repeated that I'd only seen him drive through the lot and then enter the woods on foot. And the squad car was gone. He asked if I was sure of that as well. I looked out the window. Unless he was cruising the other side of the motel, there was no car outside. Apparently the squad car scanner was malfunctioning.

The dispatcher said to remain in the room. A shiver raced through me. He asked if there was anyone else there. "Are you alone?"

"No one is with me."

He asked if there was anyone else at the motel.

"As far as I know, there's just the old man at the front desk."

The dispatcher said that no one had answered at the front desk when he'd called. He asked if the desk clerk had seen anything. I didn't know. There were no cars in the lot anymore. "There was one near the office that I think was the desk clerk's, but I'm not sure."

"So then you are completely alone?"

Before I could answer I heard the dial tone. I didn't want to think the worst. Maybe the dispatcher had unintentionally hung up. I pressed star sixty-nine and let the phone ring. Nothing. I called the police line directly. Three rings. Four. Five. More. I called again. Again. No answer. Maybe I'd been blocked by an in-coming emergency call.

I double checked the door locks. The bolt was in place, the chain was drawn. Neither made me feel secure with a full window along the same wall. I parted the curtain. The drapery reeked of cigarettes and age. My car was still the only vehicle in the lot.

Are you completely alone?

I wanted to dash for the car, but fear of whatever was in those woods kept me rooted. Would I be a fool to flee or would I regret not escaping while I had the chance?

Things would be clearer with some sleep. If I could sleep. I'd leave in the morning.

I brushed my teeth, flipped the lights, and stretched out on the bed. I stared at the phone. Wondering if the police were going to call or if I should call them. Wondering how to contact someone about Simon's condition. Wondering if I should call the hospital. Lying there I wondered about so much, but I was depleted. Everything seemed an effort. Eventually, exhaustion overcame me.

Sleep was at the end of a dark tunnel peppered with purple phosphenes. I was moving through smoke and fog, wading in a substance as warm as blood. Then swimming. Then swept along. Movement was a single direction. There was no escaping this flow. No conquering it. Although I knew resistance was pointless, I fought all the more.

I awoke confused and coated in sweat. The room was dark with only a minimal light from my phone. I rolled onto my back and tried to calm my breathing. In the stillness I heard footsteps in the lot. Echoing. A slight scrape and drag in the gait. So silent in Room 103. My focus was on the nearing footfalls. Maybe it was the police or another guest or someone with news about Simon. My gut told me otherwise. The footsteps paused outside my door. I waited for a knock or the steps to resume. Endless moments passed. The world had paused. Waiting. By now my eyes had adjusted. I saw the doorknob turn one way and then the other. Quietly. Gently. Whoever it was didn't want to be heard. Anyone without dark motives would knock.

I was sure I'd bolted and latched the door, but sometimes with a strange door, an attempt to lock instead unlocks. An unfamiliar door can cause confusion. Exhaustion can as well. At least I could see the chain in place. Something. I held my breath. Waiting. Watching the slow turn of the knob. One way. The other. Wondering, if need be, what to use as a weapon. Then stillness. I waited. The presence at the door had moved on. I felt the passing before I heard the footsteps continue down the walkway. A moment later I finally exhaled.

Now I knew why the room was darker. The lights in the parking lot had gone out. No illumination slipped around the edges of the curtain. The dark was further enhanced by unfamiliar surroundings. In the scant light of my phone, the room was little more than a medley of shadows. I found the chair near the window and parted the curtain. There were only the stars above. The moon had disappeared. As I looked towards my car, a pair of yellow eyes emerged, inches from the cracked glass. I yelped and fell back in the chair. I saw the hate in those eyes and they seemed to be searching for me.

I took my phone from the charger. A fuller light broke the darkness. The time was 3:15. The charge was at 36%. Better than the previous 20%, still not great. After a few moments, I lifted my cellphone to the window and turned the light to the glass. There was nothing there. Not anymore. Nothing but the emptiness of the lot and the ghost of my reflection in the glass. Maybe it had been my own eyes in the nicotine stained pane. I sank back into the chair. Nothing to do but wait until dawn.

I awoke and checked my phone. 6:00 AM. No messages. A sliver of light cut between the curtains and beneath the door. Dawn never looked so good. When I parted the curtains, the sunshine was blinding. The lot was empty except for my car and a plastic bag rolling across the asphalt. I washed my face and brushed my teeth. After a quick shower I changed clothes and headed for the car. The sky was a brilliant blue. Night demons hid from the light of day.

I parked hastily in front of the office. A cluster of bells announced my arrival. The room was stifling. A haze of smoke lingered. The desk was unmanned. The announcer on the overhead TV was giving the weather report. Sunny skies. Mild temperatures. I tapped the bell. The ping lingered. No response. A burnt smell was in the air. The coffee machine was empty but on. Dried remnants of the last pot coated the carafe. I turned the machine off and rang the bell again. I was desperate to leave. I needed coffee and I needed to get to the hospital and see how Simon was doing. I rang the bell again. I craned my neck to look in the back room and called hello. There was only the ongoing chatter from the television. I rang the bell a final time. Maybe the clerk was having his own emergency or had an errand to run. I couldn't worry about that. The dispatcher's words returned, "So you are completely alone?" I scribbled a note with my cellphone number. He had my credit card information. He could email a receipt.

The streets were deserted. The front door of the Coffee Hut on the corner was locked. Beside the 'Open' sign was taped a 'Be Right Back' note. I checked the door to be sure. I decided to wait in the car. A deprivation headache already dug at my temples like the talons of a carnivorous bird. Caffeine headaches only worsen until the need is met. I waited a good ten minutes, killing time flipping through photos on my phone, I paused at a picture of Simon in the tent. Simon with yellow eyes. I hadn't noticed before, but Simon didn't look frightened or in shock. His look could best be described as knowing. The photo was disturbing. I shut off my phone and looked around. Still no traffic. No one walking dogs. No kids heading to school. Lazy town. Dormant, if not dead. Waiting made me uneasy. I needed to get to the hospital and check on Simon. I'd get coffee there. Hospitals had coffee, usually shitty coffee, but at least it was caffeine.

Neither nurse at the front desk looked up with the swoosh of the front doors. Both were on the phone and turned from the entrance. At first the phones seemed like props, but as I neared I heard their low murmurings into the mouthpieces. Though they didn't acknowledge me, I was comforted to see people about. Before that I was starting to feel like the last man on the planet.

I dropped fifty cents in the coffee machine. Amidst overloud whirring some foul looking brew was spat into a cardboard cup. I lifted the splash guard and took a sip. Predictably bad, but the caffeine was welcome. The elevator pinged arrival just as I stepped before it. Simon was on the third floor. Room 313.

There was no one at the nurse's station on the third floor. So much for signing in. I went directly to the room. Simon was sitting up in bed with his hands folded on his lap. The TV wasn't on. He wasn't reading or fidgeting or looking at his phone. He was simply sitting. He looked pale, but otherwise much better. Good actually. Maybe more relaxed. He turned with a blank expression as I entered.

I tried to forget all the strangeness of the past few hours. "How are you feeling?"

The question roused him. "Fine. I feel fine. They wanted me another day for observation." His words were measured.

I asked him what they thought was wrong.

Simon said it was nothing. The doctor thought it was a reaction to an insect bite. "Probably some sort of wood tic."

I said that was crazy. "You saw it. Remember the eyes. Whatever bit you was no tic. They circled the tent."

Simon said he didn't know what I was talking about.

"You saw them."

He shook his head and said that if he'd seen anything like that, he didn't remember. "The doctor said the insect bite cause quite a fever. Maybe you were bitten as well."

"That was no insect. Whatever bit you had teeth and jaws. What about the bite on your calf. No insect did that."

"Teeth marks on my calf?" Simon pulled the blanket aside. "What teeth marks?"

"They were there. More than one. On your calf…
it wasn't just a bite, it was mauled. Chewed to the bone."

Simon offered a dramatic exhalation. "You said
you weren't accustomed to the outdoors. This whole
incident may have been tougher on you than on me. Doc
says it was just a bad reaction to…"

"A bad reaction?" I couldn't contain myself any
longer. "That doctor is a fool. He doesn't know what
he's talking about."

Simon continued, "Sorry your first camping
experience was so unpleasant."

I looked at Simon's leg. Nothing made sense.
Much of the past 36 hours was implausible. Despite all
evidence to the contrary, I had to trust what I'd seen was
true. Not overreaction. Not a hallucination. I asked
Simon if there was anyone I should call: family, friends,
work…?

He straightened the blankets. "No one needs to
know about this." He continued to stare at me.

Had he always been this distant? This much of a
stranger? Had sex blinded me? The silence between us
was unnerving. The small talk was worse. "Do you want
me to turn on the TV."

"No thanks."

The time at Simon's bedside was dragging. I
tossed my coffee into the garbage and said I needed
another cup, something not out of a machine. I was
uncomfortable. Something was off. The longer I sat there
the more obvious it became. I had to get out of that
room. Maybe I could find out more from the doctor.
There were some things I wanted to ask him. "Do you
want me to bring you a coffee?"

"No thanks."

Simon never turned down coffee. We'd met over coffee and bonded over a mutual love of it. He even had "Java" tattooed on his shoulder. His head must be pounding. Maybe the antibiotics or pain meds alleviated that. I was raised to believe there was a logical explanation for everything. That didn't quell the uneasiness in my gut. "I'll be back in a minute."

The nurse nodded when she saw me walking down the hall. She asked me how I liked the motel. "And aren't you pleased to see Simon looking so much better after his allergic reaction."

"So that's all it was?"

She nodded. She wore the same secretive smile I'd seen on Simon. Distant. Knowing. She turned to the telephone. "The police called. An officer is on his way. The police want to talk to you about the supposed incident last night."

"I didn't suppose anything."

My retort did nothing to alter her placid smile. "They may need to take you to the station for additional questioning." How was she privy to all this information? This nurse wasn't even here yesterday. At least I didn't remember her. "You seem anxious. Would you like the doctor to prescribe something for your nerves?"

That wasn't going to happen. I wasn't about to take any medication and I wasn't going to the police station. I ignored her comment and asked about coffee. She said she had some right there and handed me a cup already poured. Her smile continued to make me uneasy. I wasn't drinking anything she gave me.

Several patients stood at the doorways to their rooms, watching me with the similar bemused expressions. They resembled a poised pack of dogs waiting for a master's signal.

I should've followed my instincts and left town last night, but felt obligated because of Simon. That sense of duty was misguided. Simon was part of whatever was happening here. Maybe he'd been party to it all along. He said he came to the area every year. "Without fail." Maybe I wasn't his first new boyfriend he brought along. No telling where the truth ended and my imagination began.

The elevator dinged with another arrival. The metal doors parted. A policeman approached the desk. The officer resembled the cop who had investigated the woods last night. He bent close to the nurse on duty. More whispers. I was sure their secret was about me.

A rumble rocked the building followed by a momentary loss of power. The hall lights dimmed. In those shadowed seconds I saw the eyes of the officer and the nurse glow a familiar yellow. The patients at their doorways turned my direction. The people in this town were not who or what they purported to be.

Even before the power was fully restored, I'd quickened my pace down the hallway. The officer was following. Not hurrying, but intent and with purpose. Unworried. His footfalls slapped the floor, blending with my own. I tried to ignore the hammering in my chest. Trying to appear casual. By then my pace had quickened. I put the mug of coffee on an intern's cart. The hungry-eyed patients were still watching. Still set to pounce.

At the 'L' turn at the end of the hall, I heard the officer call, "Wait up." He tried to sound casual. Once I rounded the corner, I ran. Something sinister was afoot. I sensed it with every fiber of my being. This was not paranoia. I pressed the elevator button, but instead took the stairs, closing the door softly behind me. I took the steps two at a time. In seconds I was on the ground floor.

There was no one. I crossed the hall to a side entrance. That cop would be here soon, and he was armed. This time he might not be so casual in his approach.

Once outside, I ducked behind an air conditioner vent. Slowly. I crept towards the cars in the lot. My car was on the far side of the building, near the emergency entrance. A moment later the side door opened. The officer scanned the lot. I ducked lower. He moved down the sidewalk, crouching as he went, looking between and amongst the parked cars. Thankfully he was moving away. I had to get to my car. My cellphone was there. I could call for help. Better yet, I could leave. I'd be out of town in only a few blocks. The expressway was on the outskirts. Once I made it to the interstate, I'd drive until I needed gas and this town was nothing more than a bad memory.

First I had to make it to the car. I moved through the lot, checking for people and police as I made my way from vehicle to vehicle, trying to hide my feet behind tires. Finally my car was in view. The hood was popped and two men were bent over the engine. One of the men yanked something from motor and tossed it across the lot. The other did the same. They were disabling my car. A spark plug landed only a couple feet from where I was crouched. The cop joined them and opened the door with a Slim Jim. I knew what he was looking for. I heard a crunch as his boot heel crushed my cellphone.

The car door slammed. The hood slammed.

"He ain't going nowhere in this car now."

"Got that right. Not unless he's got a set of spark plugs on him."

The trio laughed.

"He won't be making any calls either," added the cop.

As the three men crossed the lot, the policeman clapped the others on the shoulder as if to say, well done.

More footsteps crossing the lot. Someone was moving towards me. No one was to be trusted here. Not after what I'd seen. Any slip ups could prove catastrophic. Or deadly. This entire town might be involved in whatever was going on.

I made my way to a hedge at the side of the hospital. The bushes offered coverage, but only from certain angles. I was in plain sight of anyone approaching from the side. I followed the row of bushes to the back of the building. More parked cars. Nearby was a walkway lined with benches and saplings. Across the sidewalk was a playground.

I spied a decent hiding place for the time being. The crawlspace beneath a metal playground spinner. I scrambled to the worn patch surrounding it and rolled underneath, backing up all the way to the metal grounding pole. I pulled dried leaves around me for additional coverage. I became a thing nesting. The metal canopy offered ample cover and shadow. There was a good ten feet between myself and the edge of the spinner. Plenty of room to see the feet of anyone approaching. I felt safe, at least for now. At least until dusk.

I needed a plan for getting out of town. Escaping wouldn't be easy. If the opportunity arose I could stowaway in a passing truck, though I'd seen no moving vehicles here except for the police car. I might have better luck stealing a car. People leave their cars unlocked in small towns all the time. Didn't they? Hot wiring a car couldn't be that difficult. I'd seen it done in movies and on TV countless times. If I got to a phone, I could call for help. Who would I call? What would I say?

I had no proof, only ludicrous suspicions. Offering a clear explanation of the events was impossible. First things first. For now, I needed to focus on escape.

I was unsure how long I'd been beneath the spinner when I heard the children's voices growing louder. Coming nearer. The corrugated disk above me began to move. Metal boomed as each child hopped onto the platform. I moved away from the greased center pole as it began to rotate. The spinner moved faster. Each revolution was threatening at first, the steel dipped and rose inches above my face and body. If I looked up I could become get hypnotized by the whirl.

The squeaks of the metal and squeals of the youngsters blended. The screams increased as one by one the children were thrown from the disk. This was a child's game of survival. Single-minded. Relentless. Sometimes I saw them hit the ground and scramble to their feet, running long the worn circle, gripping the handles, and trying to propel the apparatus to spin faster. They were consumed by the brutal sport of it. Some thrown children tried to reclaim a place on the spinner, but were thrown back off immediately.

After a bit, a whistle blew and the children ran to form rows along the far side of the playground. This had been recess. As the last child moved from the spinner, a ball bounced across the grass in my direction. Closer. The ball rolled beneath the spinner and came to rest in the leaves near my head. I saw the legs of a little girl running to get the ball. Her knees hit the dirt as she knelt to retrieve it. I tried to push the ball back before she could see me, but she bent just as I was reaching. She was angelic looking. Five or six years old, blue eyed and blonde. Our eyes connected. She didn't flinch at seeing me. I brought a finger to my lips and mimed shhh. She

36

offered a dimpled smile. I rolled the ball to her. She rose and skipped from the spinner. A moment later I heard her shout, "He's here. The foreigner is hiding beneath here."

"Like a dog," another child shouted.

The betrayal should not have surprised me. No one could be trusted here. I rolled from beneath the spinner and scrambled to my feet.

The children began to shout "Dog." Some made barking and howling noises.

The teacher was laughing. In a moment she gave two toots on her whistle. The children quieted. She signaled with her whistle again. This time the prolonged blare was louder, forceful enough to cause her to redden. The second signal wasn't for the children. The second time she was sounding an alarm.

As I ran I turned back. The teacher and students stood watching. On the far side of the playground was a drainage ditch littered with urban debris: branches, bottles, a shopping cart. Thinking it provided at least some cover, I scaled the sides and into the cement trough. I ran through the ditch as it curved behind a string of businesses. After about a mile it drained into a muddy river. I climbed the cement side. At the juncture of the ditch with the riverbank stood an old factory. Gray and weatherworn, shuttered and slanting, the dilapidated structure looked one storm shy of collapse. My side ached. I needed to catch my breath. This building would be a good place to rest.

A broken door along the back wall was merely leaning in place. As I moved it aside I heard the scurrying of rats. It smelled of rot and decay and the river. The central room was high beamed, filthy with dust and the debris of time. Dried glue crusted the floorboards. A metal tub lay broken amidst a jumble of rusted pipes. One wall was lined with smashed windows. The remaining glass was covered with filth and grime. I flattened myself against a wall. I kept expecting the wail of sirens or yelping bloodhounds. Maybe the police were making a sport of tracking me. I needed to keep moving. This would be no place to be when the darkness came and yellow eyes appeared.

There was a convenience store across the overgrown field, further down the riverbank. The store windows were darkened. The parking lot was empty. The place looked closed. Maybe there was food there. Food and light. Water. Supplies. Weapons? Bright streaks of dusk marked the sky. Night was coming soon.

I moved into the overgrowth of the vacant lot. The tall grass helped to conceal me. Keeping low to the ground, I moved along the river bank in the direction of the convenience store. Maybe in the morning I could build a raft and float to freedom. Movement marked the darkening sky. Bats were swooping for their evening meal.

I made my way to the rear of the shop. No pavement there, only packed dirt and the river beyond. I pushed the delivery door. Locked. The side door. Locked. Cigarette butts littered the ground. A small high window was along the cinderblock wall. I rolled a garbage drum beneath it and put a milk crate on top. With a stretch I could reach the sill. The window gave with minimal effort. Climbing through, I lowered myself inside. The employee bathroom. I stepped off the toilet and locked the window behind me. I didn't want any surprise visitors.

I went through the back room to the sales floor. I battled the impulse to retch at the stench which assaulted me. Curdled milk. Molded cheese. Meat gray with age.

This food hadn't been replenished in weeks. Otherwise, the place seemed untouched. I'd get used to the smell of rot. Not everything spoils. I grabbed a bottle of water and drank it in two swallows.

Outdoor light angled through the front windows. Glass would shield me, for now. I opened a soda, a bag of chips, and some cookies. I didn't realize how hungry I'd been. The store phone was dead. I suspected as much. I opened another water.

Dusk was falling. The sky was a bruised purple with streaks of violet and red. The bats' feeding was a swooping ballet. I located the panel of lights and made sure they were working. I kept them off for the time being. No need arousing suspicion before it was necessary. In five minutes it would be dark. I sat on the floor eating cookies and wondering how to escape. Nothing could happen until tomorrow and tomorrow was still an eternity away.

When the sun set, I flipped the overhead and outside lights. Fluorescence was never more comforting. In the light I was safe from whatever lurked in the shadows. I looked around the store for weapons. A revolver. Flares. A pitchfork. Anything. I found a couple of lighters in a drawer behind the counter. One of them was drained of butane. I found a flashlight beside the garbage can. The beam was fairly dim. Additional batteries were nowhere to be found. Inconvenient for a convenience store. Someone else must have taken the last of them.

The fluorescents began to flicker and dim. The store abruptly went black. Even the lights in the lot were extinguished. The ghost of that luminescence quickly faded. Power had been cut. I should have expected this. These demons seemed fairly intelligent.

Yellow eyes were already visible outside, moving towards the lot from the vacant field, approaching from the riverbank. Eyes like a galaxy of stars. Simon had brought me here to see them. "You'll never see stars in the city like you will out here. Unforgettable." He was right.

I fumbled for the flashlight. The eyes had multiplied and were nearing the glass. Another pair of eyes appeared inside, at the end of the aisle by the ice cream cooler. More eyes appeared at points throughout the store. There must be an entrance I didn't know about or maybe they'd been inside all the time. Lurking. Disguised by the light. Waiting for the darkness to reveal themselves.

I flipped the flashlight. Blessed light. A circle of reprieve, for the time being. The eyes vanished with the flash of illumination. I moved further into the store. Maybe there were batteries elsewhere. The beam was weak and seemed to be dimming. The light vanished momentarily, but returned when I slapped the side of the canister.

I found another flashlight in the back office. No batteries. The circle of light was no longer bright enough to make these beings vanish entirely. The eyes multiplied outside the front windows. More appeared inside as well. Lurking. Held at bay by the scant light that remained.

Dimmer.

I moved the light one way and then the other to make the eyes retreat. For every pair that vanished, two more appeared elsewhere. Never ending. Eternal as space. Infinite as stars.

More eyes appeared, their yellow glow growing brighter. The phantoms neared as the light dimmed and in a flicker, it was gone. I'd been prepared. I fumbled for a lighter. At the flicker and flash the eyes were an arm's length away. Their hunger no longer concealed. The dark emboldened them.

The flame kept them at bay, but they remained only a foot or so away. Waiting. Ready. I held the lighter's torch until the skin on my thumb begin to blister. A torch was a better solution.

I touched the flame to some newspapers near the front entrance. Once more I was alone. I fed the fire with more paper. And more until it became bright and brilliant. The smoke made my lungs ache and my eyes sting, but I was alive. I was safe from them. Dying from smoke inhalation seemed preferable to the fate that awaited from the teeth and talons of those creatures. Maybe I'd burn this convenience store and feed the flames until dawn. The flames began to lessen. Die. Paper burns so quickly.

I picked up the lighter and struck it once, twice, and a third time. Flashes. No flame. The eyes were everywhere, moving just inches away. For the first time I saw their mouths appear and open. Teeth as yellow as their eyes. Dear God. A final chance. Shaking. This time the lighter produced a flame. I was ready. I lit a torch and held it high. I fed more paper to the blaze. Paper, cardboard, anything flammable I could find. I'd make this place an inferno. I'd resurrect hell.

I heard a click... and felt my heart skip.

I knew the sound. The overhead sprinklers began to gush a spray of water. The alarm wailed. Protecting the flames was impossible. The fire of my salvation had turned into a damp heap of ash.

The eyes surrounded me. Dozens. Hundreds. Thousands. Multiplying even when I thought there could be no more. Hungry. Primed. Mouths wide. Teeth of varied shape and size. Sharp. Curved inward. Teeth that ripped meat from bone. The command was given before I heard a word.

Everything moved in slow motion. Another ballet of bats. Another night feeding. Mouths swooping and tearing as more creatures took their place. A symphony of carnage. I was being consumed, chewed, swallowed. The horror was eclipsed by the silent choreography of my own slaughter. The expected pain never came. I felt nothing. Dread had been the only drawback . I was an observer in the poetry of my own demise. Passive. Resigned. Curious. By the time I realized what was happening, it was over. I'd been picked clean.

The bit of me that remained began to slip away. Spreading, dispersing, melding with something bigger. Something infinite. I'd discovered my source. I was a stream that fed a river that fed an ocean. A larger source now compelled me. I'd become one with this symphony, this universe of stars. My will was once supreme, but now it seemed only an illusion, a curtain drawn before my potential. A drapery to mask infinity. I'd found my purpose. All mysteries became clear or fell away.

I was outside, moving in the darkness. Moving as one of many. No more me. I flowed through a great bloodstream. A step in that grand choreography. All that remained was the draw of the dark and an unrelenting hunger. I was nothing more than a desire to feed. Pure as before I was born. Once more I existed to consume.

We flowed outward, spreading beyond the outskirts of town. Many were before, above, below and behind me. Effortless to travel through the darkness, moving as loose leaves in the wind or like the wind currents themselves.

We spread like a shadow covering the countryside, moving with the night, nearing farm houses and smaller towns. Eventually reaching cities. We cannot be killed. We come from a time before time. We are the source. Light came from us. Light was a disruption of this pure darkness. Light remains the only interruption to our advancement. We cannot be stopped. Where there is light, we wait for opportunity. We are patient. Time is of no consequence. We have eternity.

THE IROQUOIS FIRE

Late December in 1903 was bitter cold in Chicago. Otto was smoking that day behind the theater in Couch Place off Dearborn, down the cobblestone from the theater's loading dock. He stood there, shoulders hunched, in a collared coat and derby, looking very well-to-do as he puffed on his cigar. He leaned forward and swiveled his head right, and then left. The wind howled down the street and around the corner. Otto turned from the gale, and that was when I was first struck by his rugged beauty. A man both delicate and masculine. A softness about the lips and eyes combined with a fullness of beard, a strong jaw, and a precise mustache.

Otto cut quite a figure. His wool trousers had a front and back crease, and his topcoat was well tailored. He had removed his gloves to smoke. His hands were slightly chapped from the cold, and clearly unfamiliar with the toil of hard labor. He probably wore gloves in warmer weather as well. The sure sign of a gentleman. When he put on his gloves, he looked up and our eyes met. I suspect I had been staring with unguarded attraction. Those eyes. Deep set. Long lashes. Seeing those eyes, I knew he was one of us. That clandestine something was unmistakable. In that moment, we exchanged a secret. Those of us who shared that look knew more about one another than most of our families and friends.

I was running out of the theater. We'd had another mandatory cast meeting that morning. Trouble seemed to be brewing, though this was comparably a trifle. Most of the hubbub was on account of the misdeeds of a few, but management saw fit to bring us all in rather than directly address those individuals regarding the issues. The procedure irked those of us who followed the rules. The run of Mr. Bluebeard wasn't breaking any records, despite the fact that we were playing in the brand new show palace theater, the Iroquois.

The Iroquois was a grand bit of heaven on Randolph between Dearborn and State. The facade was festooned with a striped awning, French-style stonework, and Corinthian columns. Eclectic. Most often described as expansive and stately. Standing in its shadow made your heart skip a beat or two. So majestic and opulent! The inside of the theater was fit for a monarch: a regal staircase, glittering chandeliers, and fancy red brocade curtains with tassels. The place harkened back to grander times. After all the barns and vaudeville houses and board flats I'd played across the Midwest, being part of a production in such a commanding place was cause enough to burst a few buttons.

Some called the Iroquois the finest theater in the world. I doubted that, since the world was an awfully vast place. There could be places in Europe and the Orient we know nothing about. But certainly, the Iroquois was the finest theater that I had ever seen. Being on that imposing stage gave even an old show dog like me butterflies. Half my home state could have been seated in the place. Looking out from the stage, the audience seemed to reach to the heavens, yet it was maintained that there wasn't a bad seat in the house. The steep design of the theater was built with that in mind. The young architect behind it had an eye for that sort of thing. Folks called Marshall a boy genius, a man destined for great things in the new century. He'd been a partner at his architecture firm since the age of 21.

In the current production at the Iroquois, I was playing one of Bluebeard's wives. Fairly basic comic drag. We called it that because of the way our skirts would drag on the floorboards. I was a good comic and had no qualms about the part. Anything for a laugh was my motto. Laughter and applause were an embrace that nothing else could replace. That was the performer in me. I learned mighty quick on the vaudeville stage to keep the crowd entertained at any cost. Whatever it took. Please them or starve, they used to say. And they said it with good reason.

Eddie Foy was headlining Mr. Bluebeard, playing Bluebeard's sister. Back stage talk was that they were paying him upwards of eight bills a week. More than a congressman. The rest of us in the cast liked to wax on about what we would do with that sort of money. Some said they'd build their own theater, and some said they would tour the continent in style. I didn't quite know what I'd do. I said I'd take Lillian Russell as my mistress. Hardly! But that was my business. As I've conveyed, I was known to say anything for a laugh. Besides, Miss Russell wasn't about to throw over Diamond Jim Brady for the likes of me.

Foy was like a god to the rest of the cast and crew, provided you saw God for nine shows a week. I understudied Mr. Foy on Thursdays and Fridays. I never worried about having to go on. Having an understudy was a safe bet for the producers, because Foy never missed a show. Never. The man prided himself on the fact and even claimed that he'd once played with a broken leg in a matinee until the final curtain call, had it set in plaster, and made the curtain for the performance that evening. He was a genuine talent who'd been traipsing the floorboards since he could walk. Some even said before. Foy always got the laughs, especially shaking his bustle as Bluebeard's sister. Some called his brand of theatrics overplay, but the audiences loved it and they were the ones buying tickets. Like I said, Foy knew the bottom line of stage work was to keep folks entertained. The highbrows and the critics can go to Hades as far as most of us were concerned.

Mr. Bluebeard was a marvel for other reasons as well. The production was more elaborate than any I'd seen, certainly more elaborate than anything else on my résumé. The sets, the lights, and the costumes were all the finest, down to the smallest detail. "A spectacle beyond compare," was what the newspapers called it, even though they were just repeating a line fed to them by the producers of the show. The production had so many dancers and sets, and even Nellie Reed doing her aerial ballet high above the audience on a trapeze. "Everything but Paul Revere on horseback," as we used to say. The awe was all about the packaging, with Foy as the icing on the cake. Truth was, this might have been a class A production, but it still seemed like gussied up vaudeville material to me. The script didn't have much punch or substance and the laughs were largely rehash. There was sure nothing much of a plot to slow the show down. Keep them laughing, keep them smiling, add a few songs and some high stepping. Light musical comedy stuff. Fine with me. That was my forte.

The payroll alone was a king's ransom. At that morning's meeting, the managers made a point of mentioning that we were being well paid in tough times, especially for stage folks. They knew we'd all seen a lot worse. And the management also made it clear that we were all replaceable. That was the truth of it, too. That was how I got the job in the first place. I replaced some louse who had the bum luck to show up late and soused. We had too much staging and whatnot to do this show drunk. The stage manager didn't tolerate any of that nonsense. Not one bit. There were about a hundred and fifty of us in the touring group alone. The cast was roundabout three hundred after you accounted for the local hires. Mr. Bluebeard, a Drury Lane extravaganza, had been on the road for a while, New York to Pittsburgh to Indianapolis to Cleveland. I was a newbie. I had joined the show in Indianapolis last month. I was still counting my lucky stars for this job and getting out of that hell hole.

The stage manager for Mr. Bluebeard was happy with me. I was a quick learner and showed up on time, which in the theatrical world meant early. I also rarely imbibed and certainly never partook prior to a performance. Once I passed the talent test, professionalism was about all he cared about. I was reliable and competent. I needn't be anything more. Foy was the star.

After playing vaudeville circuit and non-circuit venues for upwards of a decade, the idea of a steady paycheck was nice. Mr. Bluebeard had only two weekly matinees, on Wednesdays and Saturdays, and a show every night. I'd had plenty worse. Try three-a-days for a cut of the show when audiences were scarce. Playing in places with no heat and where it was so cold that a layer of ice covered the stage. I'd played towns where we were expected to march through the streets between shows to try and drum up a crowd, no matter how small. I'd had show-managers skip town overnight with the draw lining their pockets, leaving the cast stranded, once in Lexington, once in Detroit, and once in Indianapolis.

That's what I was doing in Indy when Mr. Bluebeard arrived on tour. I had vowed to do whatever it took to get a job with the company and get out of there. Truth was, I bought the man I replaced a couple whiskies after I heard he had a show that evening. I'm not proud of some of the things I've done, but I've done what I had to do. Besides, he was already drinking, I just gave him a nudge. I make no apologies. I've got no one in the world but myself.

Mr. Bluebeard was easy street compared to all those storefront theaters and fly-by-night shows. Now that I was just getting comfortable, there were rumors. People said the show wasn't doing so well, especially for how expensive it was to mount. Some whispered that the show would end here, and we might close after the holidays. Some said they were planning to revamp it with a smaller cast. The management would never tell us something like that until the actual day of the cuts. They didn't want any of us leaving before they collected the final receipts. If Mr. Bluebeard closed or my part was cut, I'd be stuck again. But being stranded in Chicago left a fellow with plenty of options, though I could do without the Chicago winter. I tried to pay no mind to rumors of the closing. I'd deal with that problem if and when I came to it. Head down and feet forward: that's how you've got to be to survive in this world. That's how I've done it anyways.

Suffice it to say, I'd been around. So, when I saw that familiar look in Otto's eyes that day outside the theater, I nodded. He nodded back. That told me right there he was approachable. Stage people aren't exactly considered reputable by the upper classes, or even most decent folk. With most inverts, class didn't matter. Sex was the great equalizer.

I couldn't help but stare at Otto's blue eyes and thick red hair. Beneath his full beard and waxed mustache, I could see the trace of a smile. So handsome. The possibility of an encounter appeared to please him. That was all the invitation I needed. I crossed the alley right then and there, thinking how happy I was to have left the theater by the back door that day and how pleased I was to have my afternoon free. No performance until this evening. Opportunity was only a few feet away. Discretion was important, but so was directness. A man had to be a little of both. Get what you need, but don't be a goose about it. A man couldn't be a fool and live this sort of life unless he wanted to end up in the madhouse. We had our tricks and our ways. I took advantage of circumstances when I could.

Carriages and the crowds passed with the holiday bustle, but most folks out in this weather moved with intent, eager to get out of the cold. Otto was an exception. I walked right over to him and said my name was Frankie. I saw him smile again and wondered if I should have said Francis. Then I realized that smile meant the formal or familiar, or even my name itself, didn't matter. He stroked his beard. The curl of his lips said it all.

I returned the smile and said, "If you wanted to get out of the blustery chill, we could grab a bite to eat. You look like you need some warming up." Like I said, I can be pretty direct when something catches my eye, and Otto had definitely done that.

"Do I?" He eyed the state of my gloves and shoes and the tattered sleeve of my overcoat. I suppose he surmised that dinner would be his treat.

I put my hands behind my back. "There are pubs and dining halls all around." I took off my cap, scratched my head, and tried to make it sound like the most natural thing in the world when I added, "Or maybe we could go over to my place for a bit. I don't have much in the way of food, but you can get warmed up there."

He smiled. "I suspect I could at that." There was a gleam in his eye. He knew the real conversation we were having and the agreement being made below the words. Maybe that was why he'd been standing in the alley smoking his cigar in the first place. Availability was another way of getting what you needed.

Otto might not have smiled if he'd known where I was living. Rosa's Rooming House was five dank floors of flophouse off Wabash in the South Loop. Walking those slanted halls, it was easy to suppose that one day in the near future the all of it would come crashing down. My room was on the fourth floor.

Otto asked if my place was safe. I knew what he meant and said that no one cared there. "At all," I added. My statement was not entirely accurate. We had to be reasonably discreet at Rosa's, after all, it wasn't a bawdy house. All the proprietor really cared about was the fact that I had steady work and paid my rent in advance. Show people had to pay up front. House rules. Rosa and her husband wouldn't tolerate my kind living there otherwise. Too great a risk. Other than that, if we practiced discretion, we were let be. With these accommodations, she couldn't afford to be climbing on any high horse over the behavior of her lodgers. I suspected Rosa herself had a past.

The producers of Mr. Bluebeard issued steady paychecks, but thirty bucks a week didn't go far. Since I liked to save a bit of my money, I took a room at Rosa's. I'd been high and dry without a dime too many times. I wouldn't be that fool again. A fellow has to be ready for a rainy day or two.

My room resembled a cubicle with only a cot, dresser, chair, pitcher, and wash basin inside. If I had five guys sharing it with me, we could have called it a dressing room. That was an old show-folk joke. The room was drafty, but I was grateful for the window. Lots of the rooms didn't have one. The window made it seem a little less like a box. We'll all end up in a box one day and I was in no rush to hurry things along. No need to bury myself above ground as well. The accommodations at Rosa's might not have been big or even considered respectable, but it was more than enough for what we had in mind, and there was no mistaking what that was. I looked over my shoulder and caught the way Otto eyed my behind as we climbed the stairs.

The wooden floors creaked as we made our way to my room. We heard voices from behind the doors, but no one was walking about. There were creaks on the floorboards above. I knew for a fact that more than a few of my fellow occupants had similar invert leanings. We were all very private. The imbibers caused a greater ruckus than we ever did. I suspect all most of us really wanted was to live our lives in peace and take our pleasures in the shadows.

Once the door closed, I turned the lock. Otto tossed his overcoat and suit coat aside and pulled me tight. We were both eager to satisfy a need for one another. He was still cold to the touch from the weather outside, but I was rapidly changing that condition. I was desperate for someone to hold. Being alone is always worse around the holidays.

The wind was howling outside. After an especially loud gale, I tried to make light of it and

whistled a bar or two of In The Good Old Summertime.
Otto silenced my foolishness by kissing me hard on the
lips until every nerve about my mouth was tingling. His
waxed mustache was softer than I had imagined, but his
beard still scratched. He undid his studs and pulled the
collar from his shirt. I felt his hardness through his
woolen trousers and drawers. He felt mine. Our pelvises
brushed and then ground together. Our mouths grew
hungrier. He slapped my behind hard and pulled the hair
at the nape of my neck to angle my head into a deeper
kiss. The roughness felt good, like want. Sometimes
there was no better feeling than being wanted like that.
Desperately. Desire had eclipsed all else.

 We heard laughter outside my door and paused a
moment. He held me with his eyes. Kissing me gently
about the neck, he cupped my buttocks, kneading them
silently, then again softly kissing me about the neck and
ears. The nubs on my chest hardened. The voices passed,
moving down the hall.

 He unbuttoned his vest and shirt. His undershirt
was an expensive blend of cotton and silk. I unbuttoned
his fly and reached inside. I felt his manhood in my hand
and the wetness as I stroked him. I pulled off my shirt
and dropped my trousers and shorts. He groped me,
playing with my behind more aggressively. Slapping my
bare buttocks, cupping the cheeks, kneading them,
spreading, spanking, exploring a bit with a finger. He
buried his face in my shoulder to stifle a moan. He liked
the feel of my rear. Otto pushed me back upon the cot
and slipped the suspenders from his shoulders. They
hung at his waist until he shifted a bit, and his trousers
fell to the floor. He slipped out of his leather shoes and
tossed his pants and drawers onto the chair beside the
cot. "Turn over," he commanded in a whisper. "Now I

want to see your backside." When I did as I was told he ordered me to get on my knees and demonstrate my want of him.

I turned onto my stomach and grabbed the flattened rag pillow. I wondered how many heads had rested there and how many passionate cries those rags had stifled. I rose on my knees and spread my buttocks. I whispered, "Please," and readied myself for a stab of penetration. None came. Instead there came a stinging spank, and then another. I shushed him. The slaps were a bit loud for this place. Otto complied and, with a wicked grin, moved between my thighs. Now he was groping, kneading, spreading. Then a lick. Another. "Please," I repeated. Begging pleased him. His tongue became busy. He was fevered but skilled. He rubbed his beard across the sensitized skin. I moaned, despite myself. "Please." Otto knew how to pleasure a man. He knew when to be aggressive and when to be gentle. He understood the power of a good teasing. We muted our passion. His moans became whispers. Our gasps were a soft rhythmic music.

"You are mine," he whispered.

Those words could mean so many things.

Amidst the howling wind and the creaking of the floorboards, we were one. His weight was substantial, ideal for grounding me in this paradise. He released himself with his head buried in the pillow beside mine. His skin reddened. The veins on his neck rose in relief. He was intense, euphoric, ruled by his release. He shook with tremors in the aftermath. Spent. Heavy. Despite the chill our bodies were dewy with sweat. Musky.

In moments, our breathing slowed. We kissed again. There was such tenderness in his eyes and in that

54

moment, the man I perceived as the real Otto was revealed.

With only a brief reprieve, we made love a second time. I suspect we'd both been deprived for too long. The first time satisfied a need. The second time we moved slower and with a greater intensity. The second time meant something more. Otto still seemed to fancy a bit of roughness. He was passionate. Exciting. I was on my back with my legs locked about him, and looked into those deep blue eyes, eyes as deep and blue as glacial lakes. So blue against pale skin. Those were eyes I shall never forget. His red hair was wild and unkempt and lay in damp curls over his forehead. "You are mine," he repeated.

The second time we joined, in that dingy room on that cold December afternoon, I saw Otto as he really was, the sweet savage behind the facade and the manners. We'd shed more than clothes. When life requires a man to hide his true nature, it is startling to see that genuine self revealed and suddenly, the loneliness that all but defined him, disappears. The feeling took my breath away. The second time we made love, I heard only the cooing of pigeons on the window ledge. They mirrored my contentment at being one with this wonderful man, at finding this port amidst a maelstrom.

Though we'd been intimate, Otto remained a mystery to me. I knew his essence, but none of the layers surrounding it, none of the ways he was known. I had no idea who he was in the world, only who he was in that room, only as the man lying beside me.

Despite knowing no particulars about Otto or his situation in life, I wanted more. This was about something greater than passion. Already I began to fancy possibilities, a future. I've heard it said that the domain of the heart is an uncharted land. Now I understood the phrase. The way I felt that afternoon as we held each other on my small cot at Rosa's was unlike anything I had known.

My head was on his furry chest. I felt his heartbeat or maybe it was my own. Both seemed the same to me. I touched his beard and his cheek and felt great peace. Otto would take care of me. I told him his heart sounded like a ticking clock and planted a trail of kisses across his hirsute chest. He yanked my head back for another deep kiss. His roughness continued to be sudden and exciting.

We were silent for the most part, at least at first. Lying in his arms I felt both safe and free. The best of both worlds. Contentment is so rare for me. We basked in this brief reprieve after hiding and lying and being other than who we were. This room was our real world. While it lasted, here was all that mattered. By then, I had lit the candle on the dresser. The flame danced in the draft, and cast our shadows upon the wall. In the shadows, there were no boundaries between us. In the shadows, we were one.

Candlelight made a strange mask of Otto's face, but I knew the man behind that visage. In the past two hours he'd grown more handsome. In the mirror's tilt I watched our reflection, a portrait of perfection fit to hang in any gallery. We were a masterpiece I shall never forget. Naked. Content. Entwined. We belonged. Otto was so strapping and hairy, so able bodied and well fed, thick limbs and hands like paws. In contrast, I was lean and pale with a hollow belly and visible ribs. In the shadowed reflection, we seemed a different species. Yet, in this bed, we were the same and in the shadows we were one. Even here, the way we were was only a matter of perspective.

He bit the end off his cigar as I played with his chest hair. Curled and dark, the thick hair narrowed a bit down his belly before fanning more at his groin and above his member, lolling heavy and spent upon his thigh. Otto kissed my head as he reached across to the dresser. He brought the flame closer to light his cigar. He said it was Cuban. I supposed it was quite expensive. Two more were in the pocket of his overcoat. A gentleman's indulgence. He did not offer me a cigar. I handed him a dish to use as an ashtray before putting my cheek back on the bristle of his chest. His free arm was stroking the hairs of my lumbar region. I continued to roam across his furry flesh with my fingers. With my head on his breast, his every utterance rumbled. His words seemed from a greater place. The aroma of the cigar filled the room and was on his breath when he kissed my forehead, my temple. He pulled me so close, I had to catch my breath.

Otto claimed to be unmarried and from out of town. He said so when he first introduced himself as Otto. Perhaps none of what he said was true. I had my suspicions. Maybe who he claimed to be during his encounters was just another part of the fantasy. Maybe it fueled his excitement, or eased his guilt. I had an actor's appreciation of role playing. In his defense, an 'O' was stitched on the kerchief he pulled from his coat pocket, the kerchief he used to clean himself. The kerchief he left behind and the kerchief I kept. In the end, who he was in the world didn't matter. I knew who he was to me. Maybe the mystery made him more attractive. Most of my partners have been anonymous. That's the way it was in this life.

Otto said he was a businessman. When I asked what sort of business, he said sales which told me nothing save for the fact that he didn't want to discuss how he made his way in the world. Or even if he earned a living. My head was still on his chest. I was still lulled by the rumble as he spoke. Being nestled in his strong arms was all that mattered. No need for me to know anything more.

I suspected Otto's primary source of income was family connections. He had the refined air of someone who'd been familiar with proper behavior since the cradle. His baby shoes were probably bronzed or dipped in gold. His class was betrayed by the trim of his beard and the curl of his mustache. No laborer would own such a fine shirt, or suit, or trousers with those labels, or a monogrammed kerchief. Even his drawers were hand stitched. His refinement made his coarse dominance during intimate relations all the more attractive, probably for both of us. He was a cultured barbarian.

He cooly smoked his cigar as he continued to stroke my back. He kissed my head and said I had pleased him. Those words may sound arrogant to some, but not to me. I waited for him to say more, but Otto did not elaborate. Pleasing him was enough.

In the wake of his brief answers, with little prompting I shared everything about myself. Afterglow had roused the magpie inside me. I spoke too quickly and too excitedly. Despite my rush of words, he continued to stroke my back and smoke in silence. After gushing my life story, I worried that Otto might suspect me of lunacy, but my nervous chatter seemed to amuse him.

I showed him the greasepaint in my cardboard suitcase and a couple of comic props I carried with me just in case. As I said, I'd been stranded on production tours more than once. I dug out the scrapbook that held all my clippings and reviews and vaudeville sheets. Frankie this and Frankie that. My name had been listed on playbills from Cleveland to Seattle to Rochester. I showed him the autographs of some of the entertainers I'd known: Lillie Langtry. Paul Dresser. Louise Dunlap. Charles Harris. Harry Davenport. I even had one of Sarah Bernhardt's handkerchiefs. I never worked with the Divine Sarah on the stage, but I told Otto that I had. I confessed I wanted to be as famous as Eddie Foy.

Otto watched me from the cot, still smoking his cigar. His free arm was bent at the elbow with one hand behind his head. A savage in repose. Though I was a decade his senior, he called me his good boy. He seemed amused by my sharing of my memorabilia. He said he admired my knowing what I wanted, and asked why in heaven's name I wanted to be famous. I told him I wanted to be known so people would look at me with respect. I said I wanted to be rich because it made life easier.

"Not always." Otto rolled the ash from his smoke. He was looking at me more than my mementos.

I should have asked him what he meant, but I refrained.

Instead of pulling back the reins on my rambling, I continued. I showed him a program from Mr. Bluebeard with my name in it. "That's why I'm here. Sure, my name is a ways down the list, but it is there, properly spelled and in black and white." I added that sometimes an actor takes on smaller roles to round out his experience. I told Otto about how grand The Iroquois Theater was inside.

Sharing my Christian name, my occupation, bits of my past, and even my current place of employment

59

was not wise. I always say that a loose tongue is a good way to lose your freedom. Incarceration in the county asylum was a fate I wouldn't wish on a dog. I knew better than to be so forthcoming, but I also knew how I felt being with him. I would have done anything to enchant him, to amuse him, to get him to see me as special. Sometimes survival in this world means more than being safe. Sometimes survival requires risk. A wise man knows when the gamble is worth it.

The afternoon slowly faded, and darkness fell outside. Life beyond that room was calling. I had a show. Although I love performing, getting off that cot and heading to the theater was so difficult. I had to move quickly. If I dawdled, I feared staying in that room forever. There were certainly worse fates. I told Otto I had a show and needed to get to the theater. With theater managers, early was the best policy. They'd keep us backstage in leg chains if they could. One less thing to worry about, I suppose. After today's cast and crew meeting, it would be foolhardy to arrive late to the theater. Tardiness today would be courting dismissal.

I asked Otto if he wanted to stay in my room until after the show or come back later. He shook his head at the suggestion. He had a meeting.

"A meeting so late in the day," I asked.

He said it was a dinner engagement. Clearly he did not like being questioned. His upper hand was as apparent as the fact that he wasn't being truthful. Touring shows as long as I have, and dealing with assorted questionable characters, I'd become skilled at being able to tell when someone wasn't being honest.

Otto owed me nothing. I had lied to men countless times. I suspected that Otto had a family. Maybe a wife and children. Maybe not. He definitely had a life outside of this room that required tending. I wondered how important that other life was to him, and how it compared with this afternoon. I suspected he felt as I did about us, but I was afraid to ask. I wondered if his home really felt like home, or like another obligation that left him feeling lonely.

I asked Otto to meet me the following day at the entrance to Couch Place. When I said it, Otto looked puzzled. I suspected he'd never encountered anyone so bold or foolish as to plan a rendezvous with him. That brand of behavior certainly wasn't common.

He shook his head. It was the name of the meeting place which confused him. Maybe he was a an out of town businessman after all. I explained that Couch Place was the name of the alley where he'd been smoking and watching passersby when I first approached him.

Making dates of this sort in advance was a good way to get arrested. The asylums were full of such cases. Foolhardy romantics. I had no guarantee that tomorrow at noon a wagon wouldn't be waiting to haul me away. I'd heard of just such things. In a rush of guilt or shame in the aftermath of an encounter, a man alerts the constables of the doings, claiming he was lured. Chance meetings were the best way to survive as an outsider. Their unplanned nature made them even more invisible to observers.

Seeing Otto again was not something I planned on leaving to fate. I knew I'd regret not trying to see this strapping man again. I said if we met tomorrow, we could spend the day together. "Right here on this cot," I added, slapping a place on the blanket beside me. I said we could make it like today. "And with a little luck, we could make it even better." His eyebrows rose. A smile appeared and again I saw the man behind the mask. He adjusted his derby but made no promises. Instead, he said it would be less noticeable if we left the rooming house separately. I nodded, though given his dapper appearance, it was obvious that Otto was a guest and not a tenant.

At the theater that night I was grinning ear to ear and whistling Bill Bailey Won't You Please Come Home. Despite the ungodly chill outside, a spring was in my step. Several fellows in the company and crew ribbed me about it, asked if I had a honey tucked away somewhere. None of them knew about me except the two cast members I had been intimate with. The theater attracts outsiders and, in my experience, that was a good way to meet willing partners. The bad part was that doing so meant having relations with someone you work with, but most of us were adept at keeping that part of our lives hidden. That was something else we did to survive in the world.

I floated through the footlights on memories of Otto. My entire performance was given in a lover's daze. I was goofy and energized and perfect. Foy himself clapped me on the back in the middle of the show and said, "Well done, Frankie." The stage manager gave me an actual grin, more than he'd ever done before. Typically he saved his smiles for Foy. Before I knew it, the final curtain had come down on the three acts and thirteen scenes in the show. A few cast mates asked if I wanted to go out afterwards. Beer and barroom cheer couldn't compare to the heady intoxication which still lingered from my afternoon. I said I was exhausted. I wanted to return to my room and feel the warmth of Otto on the blankets. I wanted to smell the scent of his cigar in the room and the heavy musk of his sweat on the blankets. I was counting the moments until I'd see him again.

The following morning, I reviewed my behavior with Otto from the day before, picking apart every indiscretion and ill chosen word. Remembering every awkward moment, I fretted he might not show. I needn't have worried. My smile widened to see Otto waiting at five minutes of noon when I approached Couch Place. This time I approached the alley from State Street. He stood and stroked his beard, watching the passing carriages and the bustle of the crowds. Watching for me. I was that beautiful man's secret, the reason he was standing there on this bitter cold December day.

Otto held a small box beneath his arm. He turned around as if knowing just when I would approach. As I neared, he turned and said in a low voice, "You lead. I want to see you walk away." A fire burned in his eyes. Lust. Hunger. Eagerness. I was thrilled to discover that he was as excited to see me as I was to see him. He simply had a different way of showing it.

The previous night, back in my room after the theater, I was restless, wondering if everything I felt when we were together was genuine or a concoction of desperation and loneliness. Those demons had tricked me when I was young and naïve. Could they trick me again? I had held his kerchief in my hand as I drifted to sleep.

The second day, when we saw one another, our eyes met as they had during the throes of passion. At that moment, I knew I was his, and that he was in love with me. Despite all else, this thing between us was that simple. Love. No one is that good an actor, not even Richard Bennett. Otto's assertion of "You're mine," echoed in my mind. His primal declaration of love.

When we got in the door of my rented room I asked what was in the box. "A gift for my nephew, a teddy bear," he replied. The new craze of stuffed bears were named in honor of President Theodore "Teddy" Roosevelt. Those bears were popular that holiday season. I wondered if the teddy was really for a nephew and not a son. I wondered what it must be like to have a family, and actually know your blood kin. All my people were dead or simply gone. By the time I was ten, they'd all scattered like dust. I'd been fending for myself ever since.

People were about the boarding house that second day. Taking extra caution, I wedged a straight-back chair beneath the knob. There was a difference between taking a risk and being a dullard. Otto smiled at the cautionary measure and tossed the gift box on the small dresser. He removed his over coat and his suit coat. He ravished me with his eyes before kissing me hard on the mouth. When he broke from the embrace, he undid his collar and pressed his forehead to mine. We stayed that way a moment. Eyes locked. Bodies touching.

As he began to undress me, muted light from the window cast a glow upon us. Frost ferns arced and climbed across the rattling glass. Otto grabbed the brim of my cap and threw it aside. He unwound my scarf and kissed the sides of my neck, up one side and down the other. He planted kisses at the nape. The tickling of his beard and mustache gave me shivers. Every nerve in my body was receptive to his maestro's touch and gentle kisses. His arms encircled me. Otto unbuttoned my shirt slowly, holding me tighter and grinding his manhood into my behind. I pushed my pelvis back to meet his movements. "Are you getting ready?" he whispered.

Holding me tightly, he unbuttoned my shirt, slipped the garment from my body, and began kissing my shoulders. His hands moved down my torso as he kissed along the line of my spine, one vertebrae at a time. He undid my trousers, button by button, while stripping off his own clothing. He trailed the leather of his belt down my torso and cracked it on the side of the bed. The snap startled me. "That might be you quite soon," he said in a guttural voice. The thought of him striking me filled me with fear and excitement. I'd never known such things to be a part of passion.

At his command of "Get down on all fours," I lowered myself to the floorboards. He knelt behind me. We were naked, but generating our own heat. He took me there on the planks as the gales whistled outside. Slapping my buttocks, his large hands then encircled my neck. Threatening and thrilling in equal measure. He pulled me back hard onto him. My knees ached. In a short time I felt his explosion inside of me. He held me so tight that I was certain he was also familiar with the loneliness of this life. I felt despair and longing in the strength of his embrace.

Afterwards, I drew the blanket from the cot to cover us. We heard creaking beyond the door and above, but we were in our own world. Our universe of pleasure was beyond anything I'd known. When our breathing calmed, I feigned a shiver, and we moved back onto the cot.

We spent all day nestled in one another's arms. Making love and talking and napping. After an exceptionally long silence, Otto asked if I feared death. "I'm only afraid of being forgotten," I said. He reminded me of what I'd said yesterday about wanting to be famous.

Otto said he'd always wanted the opposite. I kissed him and half-joking asked if he was famous already. He said that wasn't what he'd meant. Otto said expectations "of others and ourselves" can be a sort of prison. He found it intolerable to bend to the will of another.

I told him I didn't expect him to be anything other than what he was.

"How do you know what that is?" he asked. There was such pain in his voice that my heart melted.

"I don't, but it doesn't matter. Whatever you are is enough."

He took my face in his hands and kissed me hard. He told me that was why he loved me. He said those words, not me. I had been thinking them, but said nothing.

Some moments can be so ideal that it's hard to believe they're happening. The afternoon was that way. Hearing those words and feeling my great bearded man be so strong and open moved me. He stretched his mighty form. When he relaxed again, I curled up against his chest. He lit his cigar. The aroma had come to mean so much: contentment, desire, hope. There was protection in those muscled arms. Otto was my future.

Life with Otto was what I wanted. I'd always yearned to feel as I did when I looked into his eyes, and to feel the way I did when he looked into mine. Joined. United. Safe. No longer alone. Maybe that sense of being known and loved was all I really wanted from fame anyway. Otto knew me. That was enough. Fame was only the love of strangers. The love of one who knew me seemed infinitely better. I never expected to feel cherished. As an invert, I had few expectations aside from sporadic pleasures, continued survival, and a life lived alone. The possibility of this sort of joy and pleasure being anything more than fleeting was a revelation. I never imagined such a thing was possible. Otto changed all that.

Lying there, I couldn't bear to think of this as just another dalliance in a lifetime of happenstance encounters. The alchemy produced by our union was something more. Otto's words and his embrace confirmed it. He loved me. I loved him. I was his. We needed each other. Keeping this was worth any risk. We could live quietly and let the outside world see us as economizing bachelors. We would know better. The truth would lie over our threshold.

I spoke without considering my words. I hoped Otto didn't regret saying that he loved me, or that I was his boy. Perhaps those words came easily to him and always accompanied his touch. I was a decade his senior, so maybe, despite his commanding presence, he didn't understand what I meant about loneliness, but I suspect he did. His embrace revealed a wisdom beyond his years. I needed the comfort I found in those arms even more than I needed our amorous congress. If a man is lucky, he finds a blend of both in his lifetime.

Otto had to leave. He was smoothing back his hair in the mirror and whistling the ragtime melody, The Entertainer. I had to do something. I propped my head in my hand and voiced a spontaneous plan for us to get away. The two of us, starting fresh, starting elsewhere. He was buttoning his collar and caught my eye in the mirror as I continued. I suggested a warm climate, someplace where folks wouldn't be concerned with our business, or what we did. Paris and parts of New York and New Orleans were supposed to be like that.

Otto turned from the mirror. He was taken aback, or perhaps secretly thrilled, by my designs for our future. I said society was wrong. If we loved each other, it was foolhardy to do nothing about it. We'd find a way. A spark of hope registered in those magnificent blue eyes. A strong hand stroked my cheek. I told him it would be paradise to share each moment of every day. He kissed me before turning back to the mirror. I've no idea if he was humoring me or being sincere. Courage is mercurial and never easy to predict.

Still in his shirttails, Otto said he had something for me. Reaching into his overcoat, he retrieved a small box from Marshall Fields. No one had ever given me a proper present before. My family, such as it was, never celebrated holidays or birthdays. All money went for necessities. And show people never give new things which is considered bad luck, but bad luck was a good excuse when funds are tight. I lifted the lid on the box. Inside was a fine brass pocket watch on a chain. I flipped open the cover before turning it over in my hands. Otto said there wasn't time to have it properly inscribed. I held it to my ear and heard the ticking.

When I asked him what he would have had inscribed, he smiled and slapped me on the behind. He was insatiable.

A watch was an apt gift for the start of our life together. I said as much and kissed him in thanks. His mouth opened and closed as though he wanted to say something more, but hesitance rose in his eyes and the moment passed. I returned to the topic of elopement. He buttoned his vest and slipped on his drawers and trousers despite the swelling of his member. He adjusted his suspenders. After putting on his suit coat, he sat beside me on the tangle of bedsheets and blankets which we had claimed as our own. I promised that we could stretch hours like today into a lifetime. "If you come away with me I shall do my utmost to make you happy all the days of my life." I swore my complete and unconditional love.

He took my hand. I suspected he was picturing the life we could have. Abruptly, he took his hand away. The response made me imagine he'd been betrayed in the past. Deeply hurt after he'd sworn his love. I repeated that I loved him, and always would. "Nothing will change that." I leaned on his shoulder and said that together nothing could stop us. "Roommates to the world, but more to each other." He kissed me hard. The feel of his beard upon my cheeks is one I shall never forget. He grabbed my hand again, raised it to his lips, and kissed it while looking into my eyes. His lips were so soft and full. He kissed me again, harder.

"The sooner we get away from here the better," I finally said. Otto didn't argue. I assumed that meant he had a family or a business or entanglements. Perhaps I was blinded by emotion, and he was simply being felicitous. I've revisited our exchange countless times looking for some hint or meaning. At some point, it is impossible to discern the border between memory and fantasy. Windows on that day are fraught with distortions.

I suggested we elope after the Wednesday matinee. I said I didn't give a damn about staying with the show. The production had been great, but meeting him had been sublime. Mr. Bluebeard was a means to finding my true calling. "Approaching you that day in Couch Place was the most important thing I have ever done." Tomorrow that moment would be eclipsed. "Tomorrow night will be our new beginning. Tomorrow we'll leave Chicago on our greater journey."

I saw the excitement and hope in his eyes.

We held hands and kissed and agreed to meet at six tomorrow in Couch Place, the alley behind the theater where we'd first met. Having a day to prepare gave me time to clear things up financially after the three o'clock matinee. I needed to get paid by the producers and collect a few debts. We'd start off with a nice bit of money. I'd tell the stage manager I had a family emergency. I'd tell him I needed to leave for home. I'd tell him whatever was necessary. I'd tell my cronies they needed to pay me back for medical reasons. I'd say I needed an operation. I'd lied before with less motivation than starting a life with the man I loved.

The management wouldn't be pleased with my abrupt departure. However, they did say we were all replaceable. All I wanted from them was the pay that I was owed. The management of Mr. Bluebeard was better than most, tough but honest. Leaving the show in the lurch wouldn't help my name in the industry, but then, nobody had heard of me anyway. Name and reputation used to mean everything. The thought had become absurd to me. Now I only needed to be known by Otto.

I told Otto that after the show, we could catch a midnight train out of Central Station bound for New Orleans. "Starting this new life will be as easy as paying our fares." I refrained from inquiring about his finances. Starting anew for Otto might entail relinquishing great comforts and familial sacrifice. I suspected as much. I was curious about what he would bring in the one or two bags he'd be carrying. In spite of everything, he remained a mystery.

Being together was the important part. I didn't want to wake up another January 1st alone in a flophouse with my head pounding from last night's rye. I'd begun

70

plenty of years just that way, and it was no way to live. Mr. Bluebeard was a steady paycheck and I was grateful, but I wanted to be with the man I loved, heading for a new life together. I wanted 1904 to be a year of promise fulfilled.

Earlier in the day I bought Otto a prime gallery seat ticket for the show. That meant the first five rows of that upper balcony. Usually I would have been able to finagle something better, but that matinee was one of the few performances where we were completely sold out. Holiday crowds.

"Why can't I just meet you after the revue," said Otto, eyeing the ticket.

I said I wanted him to witness the beauty of the theater and the magic and awe that it can bring to people, like the segment in which Nellie Reed appeared high above the audience on her trolley wire, tossing pink carnations to the crowd below. I wanted Otto to see the lavish sets and the lighting effects and the dozens of backdrops and curtains used in the show.

Mostly, I was making brag. I wanted Otto to see my worth in the outside world and know what I was willing to sacrifice to be with him. I wanted him to want me as fully as I wanted him. Maybe after seeing Mr. Bluebeard he'd understand the allure of the stage and be drawn to it as well. Maybe that can be how we support ourselves. Show folk are more open-minded than most. And Otto was dashing, with the physique and profile of a leading man.

Wednesday was bitterly cold, but regardless of subzero temperatures, the streets remained packed with carriages and pedestrians alike. Many folks were still downtown shopping and enjoying the holiday season. The week betwixt Christmas and New Year's is like that.

71

The cloaked and hooded hoards scurried from one store to the next. Many lunched before attending Mr. Bluebeard that day. Getting downtown had become easier since the elevated train started running a few years before. I rode the commuter line the week I arrived in Chicago. The elevated train was a modest way to see large parts of the city. That fanciful excursion was only a few weeks before, yet here I was already preparing to leave this great urban sprawl upon the lake. My future was no longer about progress, but about love. My future was Otto.

The matinee of Mr. Bluebeard began like any other performance except that today every seat in the Iroquois was filled, with an additional two hundred patrons standing. Fortunately I'd purchased Otto's ticket in advance. The producers must have been over the moon with the box office. On the chalk board backstage at stage right, where the stairs led to the five floors of dressing rooms, someone had written, "Full House! December 30, 1903 - last matinee of the year." Someone else wrote "Thank goodness" beside it. Some cast members cracked that we'd have to up the pep of the show to hold the attention of all the kids out front. Half the place was children. The noise out front was deafening. The energy of the crowd was palpable. I looked through the curtain flap, but there was no way to see Otto up in the galley. I stared into the blackness behind the lights. At the time I wanted nothing more than for him to be there. Making him proud was all that mattered. Thoughts of our life together had me dizzy with anticipation, though some of that anxiety may have been the trepidation over having to tell management I was leaving the show.

The curtain rose promptly at three. The first act. The usual backstage grousing vanished the moment we stepped on stage. By this point we could all play our parts, and most other roles, in our sleep. We needed to be precise and hit our marks what with all lighting and sets and elaborate backdrops of linen and canvas. The sixteen dancers, two couples of eight, took the stage for the In the Pale Moonlight number. In order for the lighting effect of moonlight to be achieved, an extremely hot floodlight with a blue gel was used along with a gauzy drop.

I'm uncertain what happened next. I was probably watching the dancers and thinking about Otto, but in the midst of my reverie, I heard a hubbub and turned to shush whomever it was. I saw that one of the muslin backdrops across stage had been ignited by the hot arc light. Flames were climbing despite efforts of the crew to extinguish the blaze. Canisters of Kilfyre were tossed towards the fire, but the flames continued to climb higher, away from the stagehands. The blaze spread further, far above the stage, moving from one flimsy scenery flat to another in seconds. The double-octet of dancers on stage had noticed. Ash and embers and bits of burning fabric fell from above. Still the dancers continued their routine, smiling and light stepping and carrying on as cooing couples in love. The cast was full of professionals. We'd seen most everything during our stage careers. Bits of burning ash floated onto the orchestra. The musicians continued to play. The audience remained mostly oblivious or assumed the ash was another effect used in the show.

The backstage area and dressing rooms quickly filled with a black choking smoke. The stagehands finally moved to lower the asbestos curtain, but the corner of it became snagged on the right side of the stage by one of the reflector lights which had not been rolled completely back into its compartment.

By this point there were shouts and screaming backstage. Stagehands ran about, trying to rescue female members of the cast trapped on the top floors of the dressing rooms and the large dressing room beneath the stage. Panic spread to the audience. Eddie Foy stepped out of character and took the stage. He tried to calm the audience, who by now had seen larger pieces of scenery floating down upon the floorboards. People realized something was amiss. Foy was cracking jokes, trying to encourage people to exit in an orderly manner. His talk seemed to be be working, when suddenly the theater was plunged into darkness. Any semblance of order vanished amidst the screams that followed. The audience had become a mob.

A horrific cry came from Nellie Reed, who was high above the audience. The smoke and fumes must have risen, robbing her aerie of oxygen. I saw a blur of color as she plunged from her trapeze onto the audience below. The flames brought slight illumination, but enough to see her broken and lifeless form sprawled upon the seats.

In an effort to escape the backstage blaze, a panicked group opened the freight doors onto Couch Place. The theater skylight above remained shut. Later it was discovered to have been locked and bolted. When the double metal doors upon Couch Place were opened, a gust of the subzero outside air met the heated blaze and oxygen vacuum inside the theater. The combination sent the blaze inward. A sea of flame rushed beneath the snagged asbestos curtain into the audience. The deadly inferno moved in an arc over the parquet and into the dress circle and gallery. Later it was whispered, oftentimes with an accompanying "God rest their souls," that many in those front rows were incinerated beyond recognition while still in their seats. Liquified some said. That was where Otto would have been sitting. The sudden and deadly nature of it all still makes my blood run cold.

Panic ensued. Patrons stormed the exits in a mad and thundering rush. The cries. The confusion. The chaos. The crowd was consumed in a hysterical stampede for escape, and a breath of air that did not scorch the lungs. Stories afterwords painted the incomprehensible horror in the most lurid detail. Some of the exits were obscured with decoration or hidden behind the heavy brocades. Other exits opened inward with an unfamiliar unlocking system. The stairwells leading from the gallery were blocked by accordion gates. The sliding steel contraptions had been padlocked at the start of the show to prevent gallery patrons from sneaking into the parquet seats. The management had caused the death of many in their concern over section upping. The rags reported that the bodies before the locked accordions were piled six feet deep. Most of the fallen were frozen in death with desperate visages indicative of only one thought—air. Many were burned beyond recognition, but more had been trampled to death in the pandemonium.

The details came later with each account seeming more horrific than the last. That day I was in shock. Everyone was. The scene unfolding before us was too hideous to comprehend. In those moments, no one knew quite what was going on. It happened so fast. Yet, the horror had just begun.

My eyes burned from the smoke. The scorch of the heat was intense. The sound was an indistinct roar comprised of trampling and footfalls, the creak and slam of theater seats, the pop and crackle of the conflagration, and all those cries and screams. The sound of hell itself lay beyond the smoke.

A cast mate grabbed my sleeve, snapping me out of my stupor. Truthfully, I don't remember. That was told to me later. We exited the freight doors onto Couch Place. In that brick alley, some people were rushing to save those still trapped inside. Others were dazed and wandering about the cobblestone. Many were crying, some in tatters, and some burned. One girl ran around the corner onto Dearborn with her skirts ablaze.

The human debris reflected every sort of agony imaginable. I was uncertain what to do. As if on cue, two back exit doors high above the alley burst open with billows of smoke and accompanying screams. People edged onto the narrow limestone ledge, desperate, and out of their minds for air. Wanting only to escape and heedless of the height, they jumped. Some were afire. People leapt, many landing atop others, crushing them with a sickening thud, sometimes an audible crunch. In the building across the alley, several young men three stories up tried to extend a wooden plank across the abyss, but to no avail. Several cast mates and passersby gathered a tarp and some blankets as makeshift nets. I joined them. We attempted to catch people, but many were jumping in too rapid a succession to rescue. We did the best we could. I like to think we saved a few lives.

As I stood at the tarp, I wondered what had become of Otto. Had he remained in his seat during the fracas? Had he been courteous and waited for others to pass, thereby sealing his fate? I had no way of knowing. I could only hope that by some miracle he had been spared. I kept turning to look at the mouth of the alley where we had met and where he had promised to meet me again. He wasn't there. When he fled from the blaze would he look for me there or go to Rosa's? I held onto that hope as tightly as I held onto the tarp.

A fire pump and the fire-fighting crew with additional steam pumpers soon arrived. We learned later the alarm box for the theater had never been hooked up with the fire station. More negligence. I was nearly blind, my eyes were burned and tearing from the smoke. I felt the blistered skin on my face. I wiped my eyes with my sleeve and continued to look for Otto among the crowd. No others came to the doorway. Someone whispered that all left inside must be dead.

Bodies were taken from the theater by the fire crew and volunteers and were laid side by side along the sidewalk in front of the Randolph Street entrance of the theater. That grand facade, once synonymous with beauty was now more an open air charnel house. The dead stretched an entire block. The horrors on the sidewalk were worse than enduring the blaze. Some bodies lying there bore boot and heel marks. Most wore the agonized face of death. On many the clothes were burned off or had melted onto their forms. These dead were bereft of dignity. Women blackened. Children bloodied. Men often unrecognizable. The carnage was overwhelming. I trudged the length of the street. This was a vision one takes to the grave.

Some of the injured were taken to nearby restaurants, like the Sherman House and Thompson's. Many of those in agony were laid out upon the marble tabletops. Others were taken down the street to Marshall Fields. The beleaguered doctors and attending folks did their best. The din of agony was deafening. Many of the badly burned succumbed over the next few hours.

The stench of burnt flesh hung in the winter chill, causing me to sporadically gag. The phantom of that stink remained with me, accompanied by that grim memory.

I watched as a team of policemen clubbed the pickpockets scavenging among the dead. The lowest of the low.

The cries and screams of women and children were constant. Names were being called; desperately, hoarsely, in a whisper, muttered as a plea. Sometimes wails of recognition rose from the sidewalk. Sometimes cries of agony. The December wind seemed a grim accompaniment to the suffering. I fought the sting of my eyes and once again paced the already-frosting line of corpses, searching for Otto. Maybe I would recognize his coat or his derby or his gloves or his hands. I recalled those hands around me, undressing me, caressing me, coaxing me to experience greater pleasures. I remembered kissing and taking hold of those hands. I would never forget the feel of those hands upon me, but I wondered if I would ever recognize them.

Perhaps Otto had escaped. Maybe instead of going to Couch Place, he was wandering the streets looking for me. Perhaps, as I had hoped earlier, he had gone to Rosa's. Why was I looking amongst the corpses when I wanted him to be alive? I raised my collar to the cold. The horror of the day was still unreal and it all happened so fast, less than five minutes from first spark to the peak of the inferno.

I ran to Rosa's, but no one was waiting outside. No one had asked after me at the desk. I ran in circles around the Iroquois, wondering if I'd only just missed him... and was continuing to miss him. Wondering where he would be or go if he were alive. The hospitals quickly filled. I checked the facilities which had taken in the burned and injured. Otto was in none of them, provided that his real name was Otto. I hadn't the luxury of knowing his surname. My search was proving futile.

Returning from the hospitals, I passed the theater from the south side of Randolph. The sidewalk was still packed. Relatives had already taken a few of the bodies. A mother flung the bodies of her children over her shoulders and ran down the street, screaming. She slipped on a patch of ice and fell, but promptly picked up the lifeless bodies of the toddlers and continued her mad trek down Randolph. A husband lifted the corpse of his wife and carried her in his arms down the sidewalk to take her home on the train. I saw those things myself, but I heard many other stories of grief and denial.

A gawker aside me whispered that some of the corpses had been stolen by people posing as relatives, people who only wanted a purse or wallet or bit of jewelry. "A grossly heinous crime," the gawker called it. Volunteers loaded the remaining bodies onto carts, as if the days of the plague had returned.

The unidentified corpses filled the morgues. The overflow were laid out in stables and music halls and a warehouse or two. I could not go on a minute longer. I bought myself a bottle and went back to my room. Still no Otto. I needed something to keep the nightmare at bay. Several tenants at the boarding house knew I was in the show and wanted to hear about the fire. My blank blistered face silenced them before they could ask. I drank the bottle of rye in minutes and fell into a deep sleep.

I dreamt of Otto standing in Couch Place. I saw the grin beneath his mustache and the cloud of his breath on the cold December day when we met. Our moments together comprised a mosaic rather than a solid memory. In the wake of the tragedy, Otto had already become my creation. The dream darkened with the palpable feel of menace. When he looked at me, I saw something else in Otto's eyes. Light reflected. More than mere light. Flickering light. Flames. Otto vanished, and Couch Place deepened into a canyon of brick and ironwork. Screams echoed, the source invisible in the darkness. I awoke with a throbbing headache. Several of my blisters had opened and bled upon the pillow.

The full impact of yesterday hit me. Like so many, I'd lost everything, even the chance at happiness. A weight fell heavy upon my chest. I coughed and hacked in my bed. Although I produced a good amount of soot, it felt as though the cough was not from the smoke, but from the burden of what I had seen, as though my body was trying to loosen and purge the very memory.

I stumbled from my cot and went from one crowded make-shift morgue to another. I was part of a sizable and grim pilgrimage, a morbid processional in black. We all wore similar expressions and all sought the remains of loved ones, terrified that we would find them and terrified that we would not. I couldn't think about Otto without weeping. I felt at fault for his possible demise. I viewed every body recovered from the blaze, and every injured person hospitalized from the tragedy, but I never found him. Maybe he was burned beyond recognition. Maybe his family had already claimed the body. Perhaps, like many, he'd been incinerated to nothing. Ash provides few clues.

The mayor cancelled all New Year's Eve celebrations out of respect for the over six hundred souls lost in the blaze. The city began 1904 draped in black crepe and busy with funeral processions. There was no rejoicing. No toasts. No confetti. Church bells rang almost constantly for the next few days. On Saturday, most of those who perished were laid to rest. That year the bitter cold continued well into March.

I had nothing of Otto's except the monogrammed kerchief and the watch he had given me. I wondered, looking back, if he had given me the timepiece as a parting gift. Maybe he wanted what we had shared to be nothing more than two idyllic days. I wanted so much to believe he felt as I did. Perhaps I'd been too blinded by love. Maybe Otto had awakened on the day of the play with second thoughts about running away together. Maybe he never came to the theater that afternoon.

I toyed with countless theories. In one, the gentlemanly Otto offered his seat to one of the many who were standing, perhaps someone older or infirm. If that was the case, maybe today he lives in another part of the country and thinks "everyone I used to know considers me dead." I recalled his view on the expectations of others being a prison. The tragedy may have been Otto's opportunity for freedom. Once a fellow convinces the world that he's dead, he is basically reborn. Maybe the Iroquois was a chance for Otto to be someone new. That was the scenario I liked to play in my mind.

After Otto and the fire, I had no hope of a new start. How can a man forget such joy and tragedy? Otto had been my chance, and that opportunity had been snuffed out like a candle.

Liquor dulled my memories, so I continued to indulge. Nightly. Then the nights began in the afternoon and soon soaked the edges of morning light. Though it began as an escape, drink kept me mired in the offal of

81

that day. Being unsure if Otto was alive or dead, I had nothing to lay to rest. That door on the past remained open. Trying to close it felt like betrayal, moving on akin to abandonment. I dreamt of the possibility of his survival and our eventual reunion. Hope became an anchor around my neck.

People in Chicago took to calling Couch Place the valley of death. The alley was cordoned off by police for a week. A complete investigation of the fire ensued. People lost jobs. People faced prison. There were suicides. That was the talk anyway. I heard plenty as I waited beyond the barricade every day at noon for seven days, desperately hoping that Otto would show. Praying I'd see him duck into a doorway to light his cigar and searching the milling crowd for me. I waited before the valley of death for him, but he never appeared. All I heard were voices calling for justice and the moaning of the wind. By the end of the week, there was only silence. People had moved on. Most people had anyway.

The next week I found a job. Back to vaudeville in a place on the near South State. The money was lousy, but so was I. The weekly cut was enough to pay my rent at Rosa's and keep me drunk. That was all I cared about. The management of that vaudeville house wasn't what you would call picky. Over time, it became a strip club run by the mob. They needed a comic emcee. Having me on stage between each girl made it something other than a strip joint in legal jargon. They didn't care what I did or what shape I was in, so long as I was there. I still had my standards. I might have had a snootful, but I always showed up on time for a curtain.

Some nights, I saw Otto in the audience sitting beyond the footlights, sipping his drink or at the edge of my sight line dressed in his finery. He'd be smiling, and he'd light his cigar, and I'd smell it. With one whiff, we'd be back in that room at Rosa's. My head would be on his chest, and I'd be listening to the rumble of every word. Each time I saw him, I thought he'd finally returned. Each time I thought he was waiting for my set to end and the night to be over so we could climb on that train and run away together like we once dreamed. Liquor can be cruel. Otto was never there when the house lights came on.

I managed to make ends meet with that gig. Now I'm here. They call me Francis in this place. Sometimes Mr. Lemmon. The years between 1903 and today have been little more than a blur. People tell me that night at the Iroquois was 45 years and two wars ago. Too many have been lost since then to pay much mind to a theater fire anymore. All it takes to forget something like that is a generation. Sometimes not even that. Most people are eager to let it go. For me that day and Otto became fixtures.

Seems my entire life was lived in four days. Those are the only ones I think back on, anyway.

I recall those afternoons with Otto. Life never held such joy and promise. Sometimes, in my mind, I stay in that boarding room all day long. The right amount of booze will keep me there. That's what I had to do to survive in the world. That's how I've lived this long, though folks here say I won't see my next birthday. "Quit the booze, Francis," they say with the shake of the head or the wag of a finger. They don't know how it is. Booze might be killing me, but without it there is no survival.

Otto was everything I wanted. Being in his strong arms was paradise. Some people never find that joy. I pray that feeling of being held is what the hereafter will bring. I'm not a believer, but I like the idea of heaven as your finest moments for all eternity. I have no way of knowing what heaven is, but I'm getting closer to finding out every day. Maybe the next wail of the wind will be bring death's chariot. There's an old saying about death coming when you least expect it. Maybe that's how I got to be so old. Maybe I've been expecting it for too long.

I lay on my cot in this place, amidst the cries and the clatter and the stench, and remember lying with Otto on that boarding house cot, his hands smacking my behind and the deep blueness of his eyes. I recall the smell of his Cuban cigars. That's my world; not this stinking place, not this other room where I'm Francis and not Frankie.

During an outing last week, I thought I saw him for a moment. I was on a westbound bus and he was on one going east. The man in a window seat looked so much like him. I touched the glass as the busses passed. I wanted to shout, but was unable. Then he was gone. A moment later I realized it couldn't have been him. Otto would be much older.

My past and the present are no more than a symphony of ghosts. When I close my eyes, we're together again. Those moments hold the promise of eternity. The feel of him next to me and inside me, the feel of his arm wrapped about me, the softness of his lips, the sight of his manhood upon his thigh; all that is mine. As is the feel of my head resting on the rise and fall of his chest and that wonderful scratching upon my cheek. The sensation is so real, I sometimes look in the mirror for the redness. My bloodshot reflection is pale and slack. I don't recognize myself anymore.

Our time together was brief, but if I close my eyes, I can hear that December wind outside. I can see our shadows on the wall and how they became one in the candlelight. We have no lines between us or dividing us, only the lines that comprise us. Together. We live in those shadows. We will always be together there.

That's where I want to be, but the people in this place won't let me live there. I am roused, shaken awake. Dinner time, Francis. Bathroom time, Francis. Medication time, Mr. Lemmon. I am forever being brought back to this dismal room. They've no idea what they're disturbing. I've stopped trying to tell them. They've explained that no one wants to hear about Otto or the Iroquois. They don't want me there and yet, they don't want me here, either. I am something that needs tending. I am like one of the corpses outside the Iroquois, only no one is grieving and there is no one to collect me. Here, there is only indifference. I am simultaneously a man, a ghost, and an object.

I keep his kerchief beneath my pillow and hold Otto's watch tight in my hand and look out the window as the autumn leaves fall. They circle as cyclones in the courtyard. The dried leaves rise and fall and the movements sometimes seem to take shape. Sometimes I see Otto in the dance of red and orange and brown. Part of me wonders if everything is him. Maybe the wind that ruffles the dried leaves is his breath on my neck. Maybe the rumble of thunder is the sound of his voice as it echoes in his chest. I draw the curve of his body in the air before me and can almost feel his skin.

I close my eyes and kiss his cheek and smooth Otto's hair. I stroke his beard and reach for his manhood. I hear creaks on the floorboards above and a see a teddy bear in a box on the dresser. I can see our reflection in the tilted mirror. Otto smiles and turns and kisses me hard. "I'll always love you. You are mine," he whispers, kissing my head and looking back into the mirror. In that blissful fantasy we have nowhere to be. There is only the moment. No show at the Iroquois that night.

The body of 83 year-old Francis Lemmon was found in his bed at the Cook County House for the Aged and Infirm on the morning of November 24th, 1948. When the corpse was discovered, the nursing staff noted the presence of smudged ash upon the sheets and a charred scent hanging in the air. As to the state of the body, staff reported an apparent scorching along the limbs and torso as well as a singeing of the eyebrows and lashes. The swelling in Lemmon's throat indicated the muscular rupturing associated with asphyxiation and the struggle for oxygen. As a result of these and other injuries, two of the four nurses on duty swore that Lemmon appeared to have died of burns and asphyxiation, despite the fact that there appeared to be no indication of a fire in the area beyond the deceased and his bed sheet. Both women have reputable work records and served as unit nurses during the war. As a result of their experience with various army units, both women claimed they knew the stench and sight of a burn victim.

The official ruling by the staff coroner, handed down two days later, was heart failure. The puzzled coroner reported that he found no scorching of the body, no singeing of hair, and no blistering along the windpipe. The nurses maintained that what they had seen and reported upon discovering Lemmon's lifeless form was true. Hospital officials allowed the two nurses to examine the body a second time. Upon doing so, both women agreed that the various burn effects they had seen immediately following Lemmon's death were no longer apparent on the corpse. For clarification and as a matter of record, both women signed affidavits attesting that they had been mistaken in their original report. Lemmon was buried in a pauper's grave at the end of the week.

Early in the week following the burial, a patient reported seeing Lemmon from the window of the dining room, walking on the grounds through the snow. This report was confirmed by the matron in charge who added that the man, who strongly resembled Lemmon, was with a companion wearing an "old-fashioned" grey calf-length overcoat and matching bowler. Since trespassing was prohibited on hospital grounds and no patients had been granted outside privileges that day, the nurse dispatched a guard to track down the duo. Upon returning, the guard related that there were no footprints in the snow where the two men had been seen strolling, but that he had found a smoldering cigar in a snowbank nearby.

Reported sightings of Lemmon, oftentimes accompanied by a second man in formal wear, continued with an alarming regularity until the Cook County House for the Aged and Infirm was closed amidst a restructuring program during the first term of Mayor Richard J. Daley in 1956. Though no sightings since have been directly linked to the man known as Francis Lemmon, many believe that the actor and emcee still strolls the downtown Chicago area, arm in arm with his beloved. Numerous incidents have been reported to the downtown patrol as well as in neighboring precincts of characters fitting this description who "appear one moment and vanish the next." Most of these sightings have occurred along State Street between Lake and Randolph, at the entrance of the alley known as Couch Place.

I would like to acknowledge these excellent resources for information about the tragedy of the Iroquois Fire:

Nat Brandt for his fine book Chicago Death Trap: The Iroquois Theatre Fire of 1903. Copyright 2003, Southern University Press.

Anthony P. Hatch for his helpful book Tinder Box: The Iroquois Theatre Disaster of 1903. Copyright 2003, Academy Chicago Publishers.

Marshall Evertt's book The Great Chicago Theater Disaster. Copyright 1904, D.B. McCurdy, the Publishers Union of America

and

Lest We Forget: Chicago's Awful Theater Horror by the Survivors and Rescuers. Copyright 1904, D.B. McCurdy from Memorial Publishing Company.

THE LEATHER BAR MURAL,
circa 1975

I'd gone there often enough to be considered a regular. I didn't mind the label. The leather bar had become my home away from home. A fantasyland. That place couldn't be beat for a hot night out – and I'm not talking about the temperature. The testosterone fueled atmosphere inside the dark and smoky barroom had a grit that was almost palpable. The back room was even more intense.

Each night, when I walked inside, I felt a jolt. Like the air was charged and all it would take was a spark to set the place ablaze. And at the leather bar someone was always ready with a light. I liked the anticipation of action. The knowing. The feel of calm before the storm and that, at any moment, some sort of activity was primed begin. Expectancy made my palms sweat and my crotch tingle. Where would sex unfold? The back room or the bathroom or the arcade next door? Maybe someone getting some against the pinball machine or getting more than a shine from the boot black. The back room had a jail cell and a rack for inspiration. The sling in the darkest corner was put to good use most nights. I'd witnessed a full-on Crisco party there just last week. Some men liked to disappear into the pitch black room off the back bar. Vanish into the darkness. Vanish into the belly of the beast. Everything and anything went on in there. Felt but unseen. Hands. Mouths. Asses. Touching and being touched. Consumed by hands. Consumed by mouths. Consumed as a part of something greater.

I got my wallet lifted there once. Now I move my billfold to my front pocket whenever I stepped into the darkness. Every night was something. The leather bar was that sort of place.

I came to the bars for companionship and a cocktail or two, but the expectant thrill of sex was the real draw. They say it's all a matter of being in the right place at the right time. At the leather bar I knew I was in the right place. Most nights the right time was only minutes away. Anticipation was foreplay. Expectation was a mind sport. Maybe if I stayed for one more... or lingered at the urinal for a couple more shakes... or held the eye of that highway patrolman propped against the beer cases... maybe something would happen. Something always did. I wanted the best I could get. More than anything I wanted to be seen as the fantasy I dreamed of being.

Getting laid at the leather bar was easy to do if a fellow was willing. Being open minded helped, as did looking the part. I got my fair share of action there. I suppose I had it easier than most. My type rang more than a few bells. I had typical Italian good looks. Dark. Hairy. I worked with what I had and mostly wore work pants, a wife beater, denim jacket. Sometimes reflector shades. My hair was over the collar and my sideburns almost touched my thick mustache. Even had a flat boxer nose from a disagreement with a neighbor kid when I was fifteen. (I should thank that asshole someday.) Working class tough was what guys saw when they looked at me. Mechanic. Repairman. Blue collar sort of thing. I didn't go bursting bubbles by telling the truth. This world was about image and illusion. I wanted to be the fantasy. This world was a masquerade taken one step further. This was more than mere appearance. Nobody knew the truth about me. In the everyday I worked at the post office.

The leather bar dress code helped foster and define those illusions. No polos. No sweaters. No khakis. The sign above the door read: Leather, Denim, Western, or Uniform Only. That was the general rule. More of a guideline really. Sometimes the rules were bent in the direction of kink, of fantasy. Rudy, the doorman, was the enforcer. He sat on a barstool with his tattooed arms crossed over his barrel chest. Most nights he wore a leather vest. A black curtain was drawn behind him. Rudy was 6'4" and 240 pounds of solid intimidation. He turned away those unwilling to comply and play the game. He scared off giggling thrill seekers. Those sorts never made it past Rudy. Too much cologne and he stopped them right away. "Take it to the disco down the street." Natural scents were the rule here. Rudy wasn't one to compromise and his dedication was appreciated. Without him this kingdom would come crashing down. He was the guardian of this magical world.

Most of the guys who came to the leather bar were looking for something more. A reprieve from the ordinary. Enhanced reality. Enhanced sex. Sure, every week a few guys slapped on some denim or leather and managed to make it over the threshold, but they didn't last. Becoming a regular meant keeping an open mind. Maintaining the illusion. Things could get intense here. Those who stayed formed a sort of brotherhood. Respect. Camaraderie. Recognition many times of a like soul, a fellow member of the tribe. Sexual pioneers. The world had changed a great deal in the past few years. We were eager to revel in our liberation. Pleasure and excitement and hedonism were a political statement. We were celebrating freedom. Smashing tradition. Breaking taboos. This was who we were and who we dreamed of being. We were owning that identity. The underground world of being gay had become more acceptable, yet we remained on the fringes. Outsiders who chose to play in the shadows.

Many liked keeping the action on site. Safer. Less complicated. Keeping it here also fed the exhibitionists and voyeurs. Much of this world was about performance and the audience. Sex was a decadent service, a ritual. We were pagans with an offering to the sex gods. Public doings were a statement, blasting to bits the shame and the buried inhibitions. This world was a raunchy show.

I enjoyed watching the action unfold. Watching guys push their limits. Watching them test themselves. I enjoyed watching the bare-assed boot black give a shine and then some head… watching some dude in the sling take a couple dildos in preparation for the real thing… seeing the welts rise on the back of the guy getting flogged on the St. Andrew's Cross. Sometimes Christianity got it right. Martyrdom was very erotic. Domination. Submission. Group spanking. Water sports. Most of us had our limits, but more times than not, watching led to participation, even on the periphery. This place was about discovering and exploring new parts of yourself as well.

Another favorite thing about the leather bar were the murals on the wall. Those paintings on brick didn't just capture the mood, they helped create it by enhancing what this reality was capable of becoming. The murals depicted sexual tension, longing, and desire. They brought to life a primal thirst that hung in the back of my throat and only intensified with another beer or another shot. Animal. An undeniable want that became necessity. The murals awakened something deeper. Something greater. They transformed the leather bar into more than a meat market. The murals were the stained glass windows of this cathedral. The magic mirrors adorning a sorcerer's den. The murals captured the rapturous alchemy at work here. The tableau of the fantasy.

The painter of those murals was a master magician. His brush was a wand that infused this place with an electricity. Each mural featured idealized men, cruising and cavorting against a gritty backdrop. At any given moment a good number of patrons were staring at them and absently giving their crotch a squeeze. More than anything I wanted to be one of those gods adorning the walls. I wanted to enter their world and walk upon that hallowed ground. Those artist renderings turned guys on in a way that often surpassed the raunchy reality around them. I wanted to wield that power over men. The murals captured this leather bar's soul.

My favorite mural featured a sailor, a leather man, and a young hunk in tight jeans and a t-shirt. The trio stood at the mouth of a dim and dingy alley. No mistaking the kind of things that were primed to happen there.

In the mural the top button of the sailor's low hanging drawers was undone. His sandy brown hair hung a bit longer than regulation, but it sure made him look cute. Like a combination of sailor and surfer. Either way, there was no mistaking that he was a bad boy. Cocky. Prone to mischief. His head was bent to light his smoke, but he was watching. Calculating his prey. The sailor had been around. That type was always aware when a pair of eyes lingered on his biceps or his muscled thighs. He was the sort to give a look that said, "Like what you see?" Assuredness made him stand with his hips forward, pushing that exaggerated package into the night air. The bulge was an invitation, but on his terms. Maybe for a bit of green. That sailor had the smarts to know the value of what he was pushing, and the goods to back it up. He could have almost anyone he wanted, and from his expression it looked like he wanted most everyone.

A leather man stood in profile across from the sailor. He was in full regalia: skin-tight leather pants open at the crotch exposed a studded codpiece, a harness crossed the broad plates of his chest, and the metal ring was directly over his sternum. A worn biker jacket fit him like a second skin. The leather cap sat low on his brow and was crisscrossed by chains. His eyes were hidden behind reflector shades. A slight smirk was visible through his five o'clock shadow. Intimidation was his invitation. Careful what you wish for. Only self-assured men need approach. One of his heavy boots was propped behind him on a graffitied brick wall. A hand hung aside his studded codpiece. He was waiting. Patient. He had all the time in the world. A stud of that stature always did. He watched from behind his aviators. The biker was a master of the game. I knew that type. I'd wanted to be him as well, or someone like him. I longed for that brand of confidence. The biker would wait all night if necessary, but from the looks of things in the mural it didn't look like he'd be waiting long.

The young hunk was further down the alleyway, looking over his shoulder at the other two. He'd stumbled upon the scene from someplace else, but there was no mistaking that he belonged. Although he was another object of lust, he appeared a bit unsure, or maybe just distracted. The young hunk was looking back at the biker and the sailor, but was turned towards something around the corner. Something beyond the border of the wall mural. In his tight white t-shirt, the musculature of the his back was apparent. Beneath his worn jeans, the curve of his beefy ass was clear.

I'd seen that type of stud in the leather bar plenty of times. Strapping and anxious. Initially fearful, but too horny to care. They roused desires. They knew what they came for and had little time for games. Most got that body at the gym, but for the sake of fantasy maintained that it came from bailing hay. Farm boy. First time in the big city. Fantasy always trumped reality, the cardinal rule of this place. I'm John from a small town in Iowa or Indiana or Nebraska. I'm John the fantasy. Whatever scene worked. All anybody was really looking for was a little escape, a little magic. The only thing better than finding a bit of magic was being a bit of magic in the eyes of another.

A muscle stud like the one in the mural was in here a few days ago. Name was John. Of course. Not quite that built, but definitely that type. He wore something almost identical. Rudy at the door offered a grin and said "Come on in." The kid walked in wide-eyed and acting shy. Bubble butt crammed into tight fitting jeans. He grabbed a longneck and moved to the corner by the ice machine. Four beers later he was part of the action. He liked the fuss he was causing. After he got blown he stuck around. Why not? He was getting cruised and groped and propositioned. More action than a lifetime in Nebraska. I remember seeing John for last call. Some daddy probably took him home. For all I know he's bound to a bed and still learning all the things he'd come to the big city to learn.

I envied John. I envied being that desired.

On the night that everything happened, I was feeling low. I had no business being out in that sort of temper. Staying home was worse. A few weeks back I'd met a guy I really liked by the name of Bill. He pushed all my buttons and apparently I pushed his as well. The sex was fantastic. We hit it off out of bed as well. We were together nonstop for two weeks. Long enough for the fantasy hookup to fade and another fantasy to take its place, the fantasy of finding someone special.

He became Bill.

I became Alex.

We were getting to know one another.

That was nice for a change. I was walking around the entire time with a grin on my face. He knew I worked for the post office. We even went grocery shopping together. I liked Bill's company. He was sexy and made me laugh. A rare combination.

Those weeks were so unusual. I tended to not want to get too involved. Attachment complicates things. Familiarity ruins the image. Disappoints. I never had plans to settle down, but all of a sudden settling down didn't sound so bad. Eventually Bill suspected what I was thinking. Once he did, things grew complicated. The thrill he'd bargained for was gone. That's when he ended it. Nothing dramatic or spectacular, just a dinner that turned silent and awkward. Long pauses that weren't about longing. He was pulling back and that made our chemistry change. I knew what he was going to say before he opened his mouth.

I couldn't blame him. Before Bill I felt the same way. We were sexual pioneers. No one in their right mind wanted to be tied down. Not with a sexual smorgasbord at hand. I was the one out of whack. Settling down with one guy was crazy. Liberation was about thinking beyond the marriage norm and the mainstream models. The partnered guys I knew also had boyfriends and tricks. They were still exploring, still chasing fantasies. I didn't know any monogamous gay guys. I'm sure they were out there, but they weren't on my radar. This was the 1970s. Freedom was the name of the game. Bodies and love were things to be shared.

The night we broke up I went to the bar. Getting tight and getting laid both sounded good. Being someone's fantasy seemed like a cure for what ailed me. The downside was that Bill also came to the bar that night. He was talking to some scruffy-looking guy back by the pay phone. Leaning close. One arm propped on the wall above the guy's head. Bill was a master of seduction. He whispered something and started playing with the guy's hair. I figured that guy would be on his knees in a half hour. I underestimated Bill. That guy was giving him head in the back room ten minutes later. I wasn't necessarily stalking. I happened upon them when I rounded a corner. They were by the boot black chair. Bill talking dirty, encouraging the guy, slapping him a little. I loved when he did that. I must have been staring. Bill caught my eye and looked away quickly. He took the guy deeper into the shadows. I felt like an idiot.

I needed to get over this emotional crap.

I needed to forget all that.

I ordered a couple whiskey shots. Good for what ails you. Denny, the bartender, usually did a shot with me. We'd hooked up a couple times. Talk about a fantasy man! Denny was usually up for a good time and knew how to dress the part. That night he was wearing gym shorts that left little to the imagination. Some nights he tended bar in nothing but a jock strap.

That night Denny was on his allergy medicine so he couldn't do shooters with me, so I ended up downing both of them myself. I did a third and then a fourth for good measure. The alcohol took a minute to kick in.

Once it did, oh boy. Four quick shots of whiskey and a few beers and the world is a different place.

"Shit Alex, what are you getting yourself into tonight?" Denny poured me another shot.

"Looks like a whole lot of trouble," I threw another one back and slammed the empty on the bar.

I had a mighty strong buzz going already. By the time that last shot hit home the world had a halo and the bar sounds became a wall. I made my way to the can to take a piss. The urinal was a single trough. The guy beside me was checking out my equipment in the overhead mirror. I could tell he wanted me. He offered me a hit of amyl. Why not? I took a whiff. One nostril. The other. My head and heart started pounding. Amyl goes right to my rod. He reached down and started playing with me. Fuck. Tunnel vision. Dizzy. Everything became a beat. A pulse. A throb. My head. My cock. My heart. The jukebox. Sometimes poppers make me claustrophobic. I needed air. The guy shrugged. He was already eyeing the guy on the other side of him taking a piss. Maybe it wasn't me he was looking for. Maybe he was just into numbers.

I staggered back into the front room. Unsteady. Swaying. I needed something to anchor me. I figured another beer would do it. I leaned on the bar and called out for a longneck. I took a stool along the back wall and lit a smoke. I had to get myself together. I turned to my favorite mural and saw paradise spread out in front of me. Mighty fine.

Did I say that out loud?

Shit.

I tried to focus.

I was getting messy, but that was still better than feeling jilted. I stubbed out my smoke and swore I'd do whatever it took to erase the memory of Bill.

My eyes were playing games. I remember staring into that mural and wondering what it would be like to walk down that alley, and get nasty with that brand of man. Any of the three of them. I wondered what it would be like to be someone like that. To be a God and not a man. Next thing I knew I was off the stool and staggering in that direction. Never Can Say Goodbye was playing on the jukebox. I reached a hand out. Those beautiful men in the mural… those beautiful, perfect men. Me as one of them. Me as part of that world. I tripped over my boots and stumbled forward. I must have yelled. My beer bottle smashed on asphalt.

What?

I took a moment to get to my feet. I expected half the barroom to be laughing or shaking their heads. I expected Rudy to offer to call a cab. Instead, when I looked up the leather man was leaning against the wall to my right. On the other side, the sailor was lighting his cigarette. There was the sudden smell of sulfur from his match. I looked from the sailor to the leather man. It was them, but it wasn't them. I tried to shake off what I was seeing and wish the vision away. The halo of my buzz retreated. What the hell was going on? I rose to my feet.

It had been January. Now it was a summer night. At least I think it was summer. Whatever the season, in that alley the temperature was ideal. Neither too hot, nor too cold. Temperature was non-existent. The sailor grinned in my direction and took a drag on his cigarette. So fucking hot. He cupped his crotch like I suspected he would. This was crazy. I heard the scrape of the leather man sliding his boot down the brick wall behind me. He hooked a thumb in his codpiece and gave me a smoldering look. What the hell? I turned around quickly. My boots crunched on the broken glass from my beer bottle. Where had I come from? Behind me was nothing but a weathered red brick wall. A siren howled in the distance.

I had to be hallucinating. Someone put something in my drink. Or maybe that hadn't been amyl I'd whiffed. Maybe this was a dream and I was passed out in the center of the bar.

I closed and then opened my eyes. The sailor shook his head and laughed, "... as a skunk" he said with a nod to the leather man.

The leather man's smile widened. "He's going to be lots of fun."

I stared at them both and backed away. This was crazy. My mounting fear and confusion vanquished any remnants of being drunk. I moved further down the alley. The sailor and the leather man shared a laugh behind me. I turned to look at them. They remained stationary. Positioned like sentinels.

I heard the scrape of boots up ahead. I couldn't go back. I walked further down the alley, deeper into the mural. I stood at the place in the painting where one alley dead-ended into another. This was the spot in the mural where the muscled kid had stood. I was on his mark, in his shoes. Now I knew what it was that he'd been watching.

Around the corner a bearded man was bound with his arms overhead. His wrists were crossed. He was handcuffed to a rusted iron u-step embedded seven feet high on a brick wall. On the wall above his hands was the ghost of a Falstaff Beer mural. The cuffed man was buck naked except for work boots and a pair of tube

100

socks. His ass was as furry as the rest of him. He struggled to get free, but that seemed part of the performance, an enhancer of the fantasy. Red marks crossed his butt cheeks, X upon X.

In the shadows was the kid from the painting. He must've been lured by what he'd seen at the intersection of the alleys and rounded the corner. I understood the temptation. From the look on his face and the bulge in his jeans I'd say he sure looked interested. Five seconds later the muscled kid approached the bound man and knelt behind him. He leaned forward and began to kiss one reddened ass cheek and then the other. Lips lingering, melting into licks.

Behind the duo another leather man emerged. He wore nothing but boots, a jock, and a studded leather vest. He was slowly swinging his whip, the tail cutting through the air and gaining momentum. His lips thinned as the tail of the whip took flight. The crack of contact broke the silence. Leather on fabric. Leather on skin.

Again.

Again.

By the time he stopped the farm boy's t-shirt was shredded. Blood marked the torn fabric here and there. Red lines crossed his flesh and welts already rose along the surface of his back. His cries had been muffled. His face was still buried in the ass of the bound man. The leather man draped the whip across his shoulders. His feet scraped the asphalt as he approached them. He ran a leather gloved hand down the bound man's back until he reached the head of the muscle boy. When he did, the leather man pushed the kid's head deeper into the furry crack. The bound man began to gyrate. Leather man smiled. Pleasure and performance. The leather man whispered something to the kid in the shredded t-shirt.

The scene and circumstances were overwhelming. Three studs in a bona fide fantasy-scape. Despite my confusion, there was no denying my longing, no ignoring the swelling in my jeans. Electric. Behind me, the leather man and sailor remained fixed. In the same position as when I'd first seen the mural. They were grinning. What was once inviting now seemed sinister. They were bait. I had been lured, but the enticement had turned threatening. I'd done just as they had hoped. They wanted me to move further into the mural.

I turned back to the scene before me. The man in leather had lifted the muscle stud to his feet by the hair and kissed him roughly. The kid looked different. His muscles appeared more defined. Hair thicker. Jaw stronger. Dimples. With a hand, the leather man guided the muscle stud to kneel in front of the bound man. Soon the bound man's moans were audible. Moving behind the bound man, the leather man spit on his gloved hand and freed his erection from his jockstrap. He moved into position and eased forward. The bound man gasped. The leather man turned and looked at me. A lewd smile unfurled upon his lips. The look was an invitation to do more than watch.

I didn't know whether to participate or run. Instead I did nothing.

Across the alley a shirtless cowboy in boots and dungarees was on a rusted second story catwalk. Lean muscle. Sinewy. He groped his crotch and took a drag off his cigarette before flicking it to the stones below. In a low voice, he summoned a man sitting on the windowsill of an adjoining room. Another cowboy. Beefier. Bearded. The faded walls were bare. Peeling. The place looked like a seedy flophouse or a long abandoned office. A dim overhead light flickered in an upper window, revealing a room cluttered with statues, maybe mannequins. Perhaps the building housed department store overflow.

The bearded man stood and crossed the fire escape. His footfalls were soft but echoed nonetheless. As he moved into the light I could see his strong jaw, boxer's nose, and a generous mouth that promised pleasure. The leaner cowboy tilted his head to the action across the alley. After winking at the cowboy, the bearded man knelt on the cross bars of the fire escape. Leaning forward to lick the fly of the cowboy's jeans. He ran a hand across the standing man's belly, before fumbling with a heavy buckled belt. The cowboy's worn dungarees slid down his muscled thighs. The belt buckle clanked on the metal of the fire escape. The cowboy's member was ready for action. Another fantasy unfolding. The kneeling man wasted no time. The slurps were loud. Cheek slapping. Sex talk. More slurps. Faster. Determined. Assured. That man was on a mission. The cowboy's head was thrown back as his hips rocked forward. Neither man spoke. There were only rhythmic slurps and periodic moans. Both were watching the scene unfold across the alley. Both were voyeurs as well as exhibitionists.

The leather man grinned as he mounted the handcuffed man in work boots. He wrapped the tail of the whip around the man's throat. Not enough to hurt, enough to know that he could make it hurt. Enough to confirm control and convey menace. Staged danger. The bound man moaned. He'd been waiting. Every lick of the lash had been foreplay.

The muscled guy in the shredded shirt had stepped away from the scene. He seemed in a daze. I saw his dulled eyes as he staggered down the alley. He was having trouble moving as well. Heavier. The wounds on his back appeared miraculously healed. His skin glowed an unnatural white in the moonlight. His muscles were pumped and seemed larger. After a few feet, the remnants of the t-shirt fell from his body like a shed skin. A build like his needed no covering. He'd changed. Now he looked like a God. A fantasy of the flesh come to life.

I was transfixed by the scenes unfolding. In this alley and this world, I was overdressed. I tossed my jean jacket to the ground. The denim was constricting. The leather man and the man on the fire scape heard the buttons click on the pavement. Both turned and held my stare. The same blankness was in their eyes. Dead and void of emotion. They saw only desire. I replied in the universal language, a grope of my crotch. The man on the fire escape signaled me to join them. The bearded man looked my way as well. I took a step forward before stopping myself. I was confused that I'd forgotten my situation. This made no sense. I should be trying to figure out what had happened and where I was. I should be looking for a way out, a way back to the leather bar. Maybe I should look for a wall mural that reflected life from the other side.

The man on the fire escape shrugged when I walked around the drop ladder. He may have said something, but his words were indecipherable. Language had become garbled or maybe my hearing had been affected. Maybe he was tough to understand because his breathing was ragged. He was almost there. The bearded cock-sucker was about to claim his prize.

Across the alley, the leather man was too busy enjoying the handcuffed man to notice much of anything.

Periodically he gave the bound man's furry ass a leather gloved slap.

I picked up the muscled hunk's shredded t-shirt and took a whiff of the musky scent. Manly. Clean sweat, and plenty of it. Damp. The shirt smelled like a farm boy after a hard day's work. Supreme. Maybe he was the real deal after all. I stuck the shirt in my back pocket as a sexy souvenir. I needed to keep walking. Escape might be just ahead or around the next corner.

As my eyes adjusted to the dim surroundings, an entire world of shadows began to emerge. Above the buckled asphalt, brick buildings covered in soot and grime rose on either side of me. Fire escapes and assorted lines and wires cast a tangle of moon shadows across the pavement and walls. The alley had the symmetrical beauty of an intricate web.

Weeds rose from the cracks in the pavement like treetops from a world below the cement. The thought was ludicrous, but so was my being here. I kicked a piece of stone loose to see what was beneath. Just bricks. Freedom must lay elsewhere.

There were no streets that I could see, only back ways and gangways in an endless maze of alleys and nooks. Every so often shadowed steps led down to covered walkways where I sometimes glimpsed a cigarette's glow in the darkness. Crumbling stairways. Rusted metal. More storage rooms. Another room filled with statues. Sometimes I caught a whiff of pot smoke. Sweat. Piss. Sometimes I heard faint moans or a sniff of poppers or the slapping sounds of sex in the darkness. Sometimes I heard sirens. A couple times I glimpsed the dull glow of neon beyond a glass block window or saw a naked bulb above a locked or bolted door. Though much was on display here, I suspected even more was hidden from view.

There was no resolution to the situation behind me. The sexually charged atmosphere propelled me onward. Curious. Aroused. Eager to explore. The only way to move was to go deeper inside. I tried to remember what I was looking to find. I attributed my confusion to exhaustion. Once I stopped worrying about where I was going, I began to notice more.

Near a dumpster ahead was a long-haired punk smoking a cigarette. He was leaning against a phone pole in a black t-shirt and filthy tan corduroys. He looked about twenty. Old enough. Full of attitude. Thumb hooked in his one remaining belt hoop. He spat when he saw me looking his direction. He turned away as he groped the faded bulge of his pants. Bad boys are all the same. They want it, but hate that they want it. I had a weak spot for that type. He snubbed out his smoke on the side of the phone pole. Still looking away, he began unbuttoning his corduroys. He was bolder than most. One button after another. He was watching out of the corner of his eye as I approached. He wasn't as sly as he supposed. I was still a few feet away when his business sprang free. He reached down and began to pleasure himself. He was at full mast by the time I was beside him. He eyed me with contempt. All part of the game. I pushed him back against the dumpster, harder than intended. He grinned in spite of himself. The punk seemed to like it a little rough.

I kissed him hard and reached under his t-shirt to tug his nips. Wispy chest hair. He was lean. Unnaturally lean. White. So pale I could see the veins beneath his skin, even in the scant alley light. I trailed a hand down his stomach, down the trail of black hair that fanned into

106

pubes. I stared him in the eyes and kept my hand where it was. His pupils were flat. Distant. Nowhere. He seemed to be nothing more than this. This was his life. His identity. He seemed a single carnal moment. I wanted him to beg me to lower my hand a couple inches, to touch him, to stroke him. To bring him to his toes. He wasn't the type to beg, which made me want him more.

I dropped to my knees and buried my nose in his crotch. Sweat and grime. A previous trick. He smelled the way a street punk ought to smell. Rank. Man musk gets me going. This was no exception. I took a firm grip. Warm. Moist. Hard. Looked him in the eyes. Still nothing. A few strokes. Yeah. Might not register, but he liked it. A few more. Bit of a twist to my stroke. His knees buckled to meet my hand. Gave his scrotum a lick. Eggs before the main course. When it was time for the entree, I took him to the root. Relaxed. No gag. Head of my class. Flutter suction and back to the crown then again back down. Slow. Easy. Making it clear I knew all the tricks. Hands exploring his backside. Hope that looked as good as it felt. My fingers between the globes. Skinny too. I pulled back and he popped from my mouth. Flush to his belly.

I flipped him around. His hands on the brick wall. Ass back. Spreading him. Tongue at the muscled ring. Tongue inside. Assault with a delicate weapon. An oral interrogation. He was grinding against my face. Spreading them wide with my hands. Deeper. Spat on my fingers. Teasing digits adding to the sensations. A finger inside. A rush of air. In a moment the punk was offering more of himself. Another finger… or two. I was primed. I rose to maneuver. Maybe it was the moment or the company. I seemed longer and thicker. Even my balls seemed larger. My knees protested as I stood. Aching. Heavy hinged.

"Get ready," I whispered. My tongue felt thick. My voice deeper. The words dissembled into a grunt but my meaning was clear.

I heard a creak. A man was sitting on a brick windowsill across the alley. He nodded in my direction. He was watching our show. From the look of things, he approved. Knowing we had an audience aroused me more. Seemed like someone was always watching in this place. Drooling. Getting off. Approving. Nothing was private or intimate here. Not a bad thing. That was simply life within a mural.

"Give it to him," the watcher whispered. "Go on and give it to him good." Maybe I only imagined his words. His unwavering gaze and stroking hand were most eloquent.

I grabbed the punk's hips. Poised at the gateway to heaven. A moved slightly forward into a velvet vise. Pillow fist. Greased marshmallow. Best I ever felt. He winced. I paused. His breathing relaxed. His movement began asking for more.

I could see the dim light in the room behind the voyeur. His walls were blank. Wallpaper exposed beneath peeling wallpaper. Layers. Yellow age or water marks on the wall. Rust beneath. The flowering of mold. Another SRO?

Never felt anything like this punk. Pulling me deeper. A soft ruthless milking. Before I knew it, I was pile driving him, lost in the pleasure and the motion. I felt enormous. Sweat made my chest to glow and coated his back. Perspiration ran down our legs. The sweat between us acted as a lubricant and a cement, greasing and binding. Making us grip and move like the gears of a machine with a sole function. A single destination. His hands bled, skinned from scraping cement. I fumbled to grip the bones of his hips. Graffiti symbols I'd never seen before covered the wall. A warning more than a threat. Desperate angles. An unnamed danger. Warning with a concealed message. I heard the man on the window sill behind us. Louder. Closer.

The punk's moans shortened and shallowed into a pant that didn't sound quite human. He stiffened. Pale skin made him seem almost a statue. A Deco sylph for a moment. Frozen and then alive. Spasms coursed through him. Electric inside and out. He yelled and punched the brick wall. Again. A third time. I heard the crunch of the bones in his hand. He didn't flinch.

I heard distant sirens again.

My breath quickened. My knees locked. Close. So close. And then, there. The little death. Mortality never felt so good. The voyeur on the window sill made a comment I didn't understand and then a sound I didn't recognize. Maybe I was the one making strange sounds. I slumped onto the punk's back.

A moment later he hiked up his pants. And slid the buckle into place. Now there were words. His voice sounded strange after the prolonged silence. Was he actually speaking? "I ain't seen you around here before."

I told him I was new. New? Visiting? I didn't have the words or know what to say. I didn't understand it myself.

He said he could tell that much.

I asked his name.

"We're not much on names here. What's the point?" He scratched his shaggy hair and seemed amused that I'd asked. Maybe he was kidding because then he asked mine. I stared as he lit another cigarette. My head felt dull. Blocked. Dense with something that was not me. I couldn't remember my name.

The punk offered a crooked toothed grin. "Welcome to the neighborhood." I couldn't find words. There was nothing more to say anyway. In a moment we went in separate directions.

I wondered about our discourse. Did I imagine it? Even if I had, something was terribly wrong. I couldn't remember my name. The secret seemed hidden beyond a wall in my brain. I checked my wallet. All I had was cash. No I.D. Nothing made sense. I was unsettled, but not as disturbed as I should have been.

Near the mouth of the alley, I stumbled over something. At first, I thought it was a stone. The object rolled over the uneven pavement, settling beneath the naked light outside a freight door. Looking closer to finally see the white stone hand of a statue.

Sirens again. Closer.

Panic seized me. My legs were stiff, but I managed to run back to where I thought I'd been. More confusion. I must have gone the wrong way or gotten turned around. The alley where I'd seen the punk was no longer there. The configuration of buildings had changed. No phone pole stood at the end of the back way. I didn't think we had moved, but my mind felt so heavy. The only other explanation was that the architecture shifted. Nothing was clear.

For a moment I forgot why I'd run. Sirens. But now there was only silence. I turned to the man on the window sill. There were no windows above me. Solid brick. Only a narrow gangway behind me. Another bisecting alley lay ahead. I saw another broken bit… a finger. I remembered there had been a hand. Then another piece… an ear. Stone fragments were scattered

110

on either side of the alley. Once I began seeing the fragments, I saw them everywhere. Rubble composed of shattered torsos and legs. The textured stone of a scalp. A nose. The ridges of toes. And the powdered remnants when the destruction was complete. The powder that was probably filling my lungs, and filling me.

A faint glow was visible from the intersecting alleys ahead. I heard the buzz of neon.

As I approached I noticed another row of garbage cans and saw some peripheral movement. Confusion had me on edge. I turned to the side. Handsome Italian guy. Cruising me. I grinned then looked again. Beside the trash was a cracked full length mirror. I moved an arm and turned my head to see my movements mimicked in the reflection. Me. Yet not me. The wife beater. The jeans. The sideburns and mustache were all me. The slight spare tire was gone. Biceps were inflated. My shoulders had broadened. My waist was smaller. Pecs chiseled. Nips clear. Ass higher, rounder. Crotch more pronounced. I was even taller. The reflected image was an idealized me. An aspiration in glass. I'd always wanted to look this way, but knew I never could. I'd become the fantasy I'd always wanted to project. I was surprised to remember how I'd been. I liked the new me, but there was so much I didn't like about this place. Details were hard to recall. More white rubble at the base of the mirror. I remembered.

I heard the shuffle of feet and a voice. I smelled his cigar before I saw its glow. A bearded daddy leaned against a wall. He was being serviced by his boy. The man was big and brawny and wore a feed cap. The cigar was clamped in a corner of his mouth. His flannel shirt was unbuttoned all the way down, displaying a heavily muscled chest and stomach covered in a thick pelt of red hair. Jeans puddled over construction boots. A younger guy was kneeling before him in a black jock. A stalk of weeds broke through the asphalt near his sneakers.

The daddy had his eyes closed. Head back. Massive hands gripped either side of the young man's head. Guiding him. Verbal encouragement guided him as well. A puff of smoke. A hand petting his boy's head. The kneeling man was the muscle stud from the alley. From the mural. Flashes. His sweaty shirt was still in my rear pocket. The man in the mural. The leather bar.

But how...

The muscle daddy offered a guttural monologue, "Oh Baby, you like doing that don't you. Just like that. You know what I like. You got the sweetest way of making it all good..."

The kid in the black jockstrap pulled his equipment out of the cotton pouch. Intent. Working with mouth and hand. Focused. Entranced. Pleasuring himself and another. I stepped forward.

Another puff of smoke rose from the cigar. The daddy caught my eye. He knew I'd been watching, but didn't care. Probably turned him on even more. Exhibitionism and voyeurism seemed the norm here. This place was populated by spectators and performers.

The daddy reached down, patted his boy on the head, and took another drag of his stogie.

A man appeared beside me. Bald. Mostly hidden in the shadows. The cherry of his joint glowed in the darkness. He offered me a hit. Nice. Smooth. Good stuff. The bald guy had patches on his motorcycle jacket. Clubs. Runs. Dozens of them. He was shirtless beneath. Solid build. After a couple more tokes he sank to his knees and began to lick the crotch of my jeans. I made a move to stop him, but his look said he needed it bad.

112

Getting lucky was mighty easy around here. So easy that it was hard to recall any other way.

He unzipped my fly. Now he was no longer in shadow. Looking up, his eyes flashed green. Lips rolled over his teeth. Large. Canine. Exposed through the webbed rot of a cheek. Shit! I pushed him away. Zipped my pants. The man crawled across the alley towards the daddy and his boy. His talons clicked on the pavement. Had he been that way all along. As if he'd heard me, the man-beast turned and smiled. He mouthed something that looked like Forever. The rot made his grin all the more sinister. He ran his claws across the kneeling man's shoulder. Five lines appeared. Musical bar for a composition in blood.

The red-haired daddy looked to me and smiled. "We got ourselves a regular audience."

Voices above. Maybe just thoughts. Someone shouted, "Never. I'll never go there." Something was falling from the top of the building. A statue shattered to the left of me. The torso was cracked, but mostly intact. The limbs broke off and scattered in several directions. The neck snapped upon impact. The stone head bounced off the brick wall and came to a rest at my feet. The eyes were open. Whatever life force the statue contained was fading fast. Drooping lids. Eyes dimming. The lips parted. Words emerged. Slow. Painful. "Leave. Leave while there's still time." Eyelids closed. Lips stilled. Nothing more.

Voices. Above, the silhouettes of two men looked down over the rooftop. I heard the crackle of a radio. Police? The transmitted words made no sense.

Across the alley the man beast was feasting on the flesh of the muscle man. The hunk was oblivious, still kneeling before the daddy. Nothing made sense. No one was acting as I thought they should be behaving. The man beast smiled my way and licked a trace of blood from his lips. I ran down an adjoining alley. Down another. Another. Everything was new again. Change location and change circumstances. The statue's warning and the hunger of the feeder began to fade. Memories here were thin as a mist. Distraction was everywhere. After another turn I'd forgotten why I was running and slowed to a walk.

I'd been walking for a while when I noticed the alley ahead had no outlet. At the end was the loading dock for a warehouse. A truck was backed into place before it, but no work appeared to be going on. Everything looked shuttered. Closed down, but not deserted. I heard sounds from inside the truck. Sounds of passion. Abandon. Fornication. I climbed the rusted metal side steps of the dock. Assorted greenery had taken root in the stone. On one step, a sapling was splitting the cement. The rear hatch of the semi-trailer was unlatched and raised three feet from the flatbed deck. The sounds were inside. I crouched low. A blast of stale air and heat struck me. The scent of man sex was unmistakable. Nothing was visible, only impenetrable blackness. The sound of moans. Slurps. The rhythm of flesh on flesh. The half raised door was my invitation. I ducked into the darkness. I switched my wallet from the back pocket to the front. Ghost of a memory. I'd done this before under similar circumstances, but couldn't recall where or when.

Twenty degrees warmer inside. The floor was sticky. The sounds of sex echoed on the metal walls. Smells were plentiful. Fucking. Poppers. Sweat. Sperm. The smell of many men getting it on for a long time. I wondered if the truck was permanently docked here. Moored for endless encounters. Moving into the

darkness hands groped me. Ass. Crotch. Everywhere.
The blind desire felt good. Wanting me. Wanting it. I
was giving myself over to something instead of someone.
I was being consumed by desire. A sacrifice of the flesh.
My eyes hadn't adjusted. Perhaps there was no
acclimating to this darkness. The gray outside light from
beneath the back door was obscured by a tangle of
bodies. Maybe I'd gotten turned around. The air was
suddenly so dense. Pressing my lungs. Making me
struggle. Too much. I felt dizzy. Everywhere I moved --
more hands, more arms, more limbs. Lips and grinding
hips. I felt them. Heard them breathing and grunting.
Low whispers. Men on the floor. Men standing. Men
reaching. Men leaning against the sides of the semi-
trailer. Men consumed by lust. I found a space along a
wall. A starting point. If I made my way around,
eventually I'd return to the unlatched back door.

Before going six feet I heard the sirens. Nearer.
Louder. Closer every second. Inside the semi-trailer there
was wild scrambling. Lust became panic. Genuine fear.
The door rolled open directly behind me. Someone
whispered, "You do not want to get caught by the cops
around here." I scrambled towards the light. My legs felt
like lead. Heavy. Aching. Exhausted. The sirens slowed,
then stopped.

A cop on a bullhorn said it was a raid. Searchlights
cut the darkness. They alley was no longer a dead-end. A
squad car light bar and cherry top flashed at either end of
the back way. Most who ran were nabbed by a half
dozen officers and shoved into paddy wagons. Some men
in flight scrambled up ladders and fire escapes to
rooftops. The cops kept their lights on them and
demanded surrender, or else... annihilation. The warnings
were ignored. Shots were fired, the sound cracking the

chaos. Bodies fell to the pavement. Hitting the asphalt, they shattered like plaster. Flesh to rubble.

The distraction was my opportunity. Jumping to the ground, I rolled beneath the semi, cowering behind a massive tire. Broken man parts were here as well. From tonight? From before? Maybe these raids were common. Search lights cut the night, scanning the area for more men in flight. The cop at the bullhorn called for the surrender of all undesirables. They meant men like me. Ironic to be called the opposite of what you were. I'd never felt more desired.

A team of cops approached and entered the truck. The booming of boots on metal echoed in the hollows of the cab. I heard one of them mutter, "Disgusting animals."

They began to remove statue after statue from the truck. Dozens were taken from the trailer where I had just experienced the touch and smell and sound of men having sex. Real men. Live men. Flesh and blood men. Footsteps and more cops boarding in teams to load the plaster men onto a waiting truck. Some dropped and shattered. When these mishaps occurred, the transporters simply laughed. More footfalls as they walked the length of the truck bed. Voices echoed in the cavernous space. "More are starting to run."

"Give them time. Besides, there's enough here to make quota."

"The undesirables were having themselves a real party."

"No doubt about it.

Another transporter cop slapped the side of the wagon and shouted from the mouth of the alley, "Full up here. All we have room for tonight."

Two men in the truck trailer said they didn't see the one that had been causing problems.

"Must still be out there."

Listening to their overhead advance, I noticed a guy crouched beside another tire. Another one who had run. Fear registered in his eyes. Was he the one causing problems? We remained silent and still. The cops hopped onto the loading dock and called "All clear" to those at the end of the alley. Moments later we heard the paddy wagons and cargo trucks leave, but the lights from a couple remaining squad cars still cut the night.

"Okay, you two," said one of the cops. I thought they meant us, but each cop had found himself another live man in hiding.

"What do you want from us?" mumbled one of the captured.

The cops laughed. "Nothing you weren't already doing. Better than going to the warehouse."

The partner added, "You can say that again."

The men dropped to their knees on one side of the truck. I heard the undoing of buckles and belts. The hum of zippers. The hiding man and I watched each other.

The moans and grunts began to escalate. Culminating. Almost immediately followed by two thuds. Blood ran across the pavement. Lots of blood. Blood stream becoming a blood river, flowing to where I was crouched. Nearing my shoes. Ready to mark me before it abruptly dried to dust, becoming the white powder that coated this world.

I had to get out of here. My hiding mate sensed my need and shook his head no, but it was too late. I dropped and rolled to the opposite side of the semi. Once I was on my feet I started to run. I felt heavy, as though I was moving in slow motion. Now just one cop car crowned the alley. I suspected it was the two who'd been busy "interrogating."

I rounded the squad car and ran in the opposite direction. One foot dragging. Scraping cement. When I turned there was no hint of the blue light bar. I stopped and with my hands to my thighs, tried to catch my breath. I felt my wallet in my front pocket and moved it back. Another memory shadow. A flash and hint of something, free of context. A cigarette might jog my memory.

Ahead was laughter and the buzz of neon. A back door was open. A trapezoid of blue light spilled from the doorway into the night. Neon red: Tattoo Parlor. Neon blue: Servicemen Welcome.

The hum of a tattoo gun. A sailor, still in his white cap, was lying on an upholstered table. His drawers were around his knees. The tattoo artist was inking something on an ass cheek. The sailor was laughing and calling out to a buddy seated on a chair by the back door. "You're crazy," the waiting sailor responded. They'd had a few drinks. The service stud on the table leapt up and turned his ass to his buddy. On one cheek was a shamrock. The skin was red and raised around the inking.

The buddy was laughing so hard he doubled forward. "You actually did it, you crazy son of a bitch."

The swabbie kept flashing that freshly inked ass, "Told you I would." He tossed some bills on the table before the shipmates stumbled out the door. They were so rubber legged they were practically holding each other up. The tattooed sailor pinned the other against the brick wall, holding his arms overheard. He leaned close. They were torso to torso. Sweet friction. That rubbing starts fires. He kissed his bud hard. He didn't need a shamrock to get lucky.

118

The sailors flipped positions. The swab who'd been waiting hiked up his buddy's white shirt, exposing a lean muscled chest. He punched his tits and clamped some chest muscle before taking a nip in his mouth. The other wrapped a loose arm around his pal's head and slipped his other hand down the low back of the sailor's white pants. They rolled along the red brick wall, salt over salt over salt over salt. Eventually they rounded a corner, moving deeper into the shadows. I wasn't going to miss this. I had a thing for sailors, especially ones in uniform and especially when they were getting it on with each other.

The inked one began biting the sides of his buddy's neck. His white hat fell to the ground. Instead of putting it back on, he rubbed the bristle of his crew cut over his pal's skin. That looked to be driving the other one wild. The inked sailor pinned his shipmate against the wall, dropped to his knees, and began undoing the fly buttons. His fingers fumbled with excitement and need.

Having someone like that would be nice. Someone special to feel that eager about and hungry for. They were clearly in love, even if they didn't use the word. I got another flash of something tucked in my mind. Another ghost from another time. Him. Me. Together. Just a flash of us. Then it was over. I remembered the pain and the need to numb it. I was still hidden. Still watching the sailors carry on. But their image blended with the image of myself and another guy.

"Make it last Bill," said one of the seamen.

That name. Him. Bill. I must have said it aloud. The sailors looked my way. "Holy shit." They looked as though they'd seen a ghost, a monster, or something inhuman. Maybe I was all of the above. They hoisted their pants and ran down the alley still unbuttoned.

I remembered the bar and the drinks and the mural and staggering from there to here.

I tried to move. Something was very wrong. I was locked in place. Legs immobile. Unresponsive. Leaden. My torso refused to twist or turn. My arms ached with their weight. Dead. Unresponsive. My breathing had shallowed. Wisps of air. The inhalation was more the ghost of a habit than a necessity. Mouth so dry. Chalky. I feared I has having a stroke. My fingers were frozen. My hands were white. I was the whitest of stone.

Distant sirens approached. The high pitched howl slowed and stopped with a choked final wail. A second of silence followed, then the dual slamming of doors, hurried footsteps. Voices. Nearer. On either side of me.

One man took hold of the left side. "Been after this undesirable for a while."

I was an undesirable. All I'd ever wanted to be was the opposite.

"He's through causing problems."

More confusion. Had I done something I had forgotten, or was I a problem because of who or what I was? Questions plagued me, but no answers were forthcoming.

One transporter spoke, "He's not going anywhere... Or maybe just one place."

They hefted the husk that I'd become back to the truck. Flipping the lever lock, they rolled open the storage door. More like me were inside. Many more. Dozens. Statues propped one against the other.

"This makes us full up." The first worker slammed the door of the wagon and flipped the lock. "This shipment goes to Stockade 16." He said with a slap to the side of the truck. "Hopefully that's the last of them for a while."

"Coming where they don't belong, not respecting things, ignoring rules. Especially that one," he indicated me.

Me?

"Should've know better."

"Look, but don't touch." One mover pulled the rope to lower the door.

My crime was crossing the line from voyeur to participant. The tryst with that punk in the alley must've sealed my fate and made me a threat. Was there something else? Had I seen too much? I wondered if those crowded around me were criminals too. Maybe their only crime was seeking desire or being in this world. Were we all strangers in a land that felt like home? Maybe our crime was simply having a separate origin. Trespassers. Foreigners. Immigrants. Dirty words for wanting something better.

Knowing more might lead to discovering how to shed this shell and finding a way back. Unfortunately, once the truck engine rumbled to life, the remainder of the transporters' conversation was indecipherable.

The drivers took us to a warehouse. En route, when the van paused, I could hear the whispers and prayers of the other statues. Murmurs. Soft sighs with words attached. Dreamlike. Reflecting my own misty mumblings. Maybe they were only phantom thoughts. Consciousness ebbed and flowed. Time was a notion. Eventually the back door rolled open.

I was moved on a dolly and was packed body to body in a freight elevator. Touch was something distant. Real feeling had abandoned me. The whispers of the others ceased. Perhaps they were aware of what was happening and feared what might happen next.

We were moved to a cavernous room. Industrial. Raw flooring and unfinished walls. Exposed pipes and ductwork. High beamed ceiling. Dusty. Only statues corner to corner. An open air cemetery. We were our own headstones. Herein lies… hundreds of stone men. Thousands. Stockade 16. Indicating similar places. At least 15 others. Criminals and undesirables in storage. Quarantined from alleys and interaction. Quarantined from infecting the masses. Maybe millions were in these rooms, collecting time and collecting dust. I didn't care much about the scope of this. I was selfish. I cared about myself.

Finished with moving the last of us, the movers shut off the lights. The elevator clanked with its descent. The transporter voices faded as the moans rose about the room. The others had been frightened to speak. Someone whispered that eventually your mind will stagnate and shrink into a hardened pit. Dead. Atrophied. Inflexible as chalk. "When your mind becomes stone, you're theirs forever."

So they had heard.

The thought of my brain becoming stone was horrific. Unfathomable to consider an end without end. I'd heard enough. I was no longer curious. I didn't want theory and I had no hunger for details. Fate was easier without specifics. Charting my descent to oblivion held no appeal. Some felt differently. Some were curious. Some pleaded to hear what others had heard. Then what. And then what.

I tried to block every utterance, but the words seeped inside. Words like dullness and narrowing and atrophy. A string of words that ended with the final word, nothing. I kept reciting that it was hearsay, but those words took root. Dullness. Narrowing. Atrophy. Nothing. Nothing. Nothing.

I understood why so many had leapt from heights to shatter. Anything to escape a fate of forever without consciousness, an eternity void of use. We were mindless bodies of stone in storage, fragments in the collection of an unknown hoarder. I'd jump if I still could. I'd rather be pieces and powder. Annihilation had to be preferable. Dignity trumped the drive to be. But the truth came too late to matter.

At least my final resting place was near a window. A tomb with a view. Locked in a stone shell where inches might as well have been miles. I saw the dark alley where I once roamed, lurked, and prowled. The place where I reveled in distraction.

The alley was the lure to a place where desire occurred endlessly. A place with pleasures recurrent and where fantasy was at every turn. But perfection is a state with no moving parts. No beating heart. Nothing deeper than a grin or sneer. A masterpiece matted, framed, and hung. No room for improvement or decay. Now both were impossible. I'm an ant in amber. This world within the mural was as effective as the sweet stickiness of a roach motel.

From my window, the alley had returned to what I'd expected all along. The mural on brick was the one I'd sought since my arrival. Pictured was a leather bar scene, a couple half naked bartenders in leather vests and arm bands. Asses hanging out of chaps. Five o'clock shadows. Mustaches. Each with a grin. Both facing me. Imperfect, but real. Beside them a boot black chair with a daddy seated there, his calf high boots being licked clean. The stockade and St. Andrew's cross in the background. Real men in a fantasy world. The combination never looked better. The bar was Sodom and Gomorrah to some. A freak show to others. To me it was home.

Why had I wished for something better? Something ideal. I'd brought this upon myself. Being eternally desired came at a cost. Chasing perfection was a fool's quest.

I stood, trapped in a sarcophagus. Consciousness dimming. Little more than a thing. Immune to the ravages of time. Immune to most everything, including life. Something to be owned, stored, forgotten. I tried to keep thinking, keep remembering, keep imagining, but it was so hard. Like diving deeper with lungs and head set to explode from the pressure. If only I were free to do it all again. If only...

No more whispers in the room. Only distant sirens. Lessening to a buffered silence. The world was dimming. This tunnel was becoming a pinpoint. There was no longer the room. No longer the window. No longer the alley. The mural was all that remained. The colors had begun to muddy and gray and the borders blurred. My thoughts slowed to a stillness on every side. A stillness moving closer. Blackness nearing like spilled ink poised to swallow me whole.

The mural.

A window.

Then black.

Timeless.

Silent.

A void.

Sound returning. Faint at first and then louder.

I lay on the leather bar floor a moment, unsure of what happened. The black cement was sticky, filthy with spilled beer and who knew what else. Was I crying? Someone grabbed the back of my jeans and hoisted me to my feet.

"I can move."

Rudy the doorman eyed me suspiciously. "Alex, you had a little too much fun tonight."

He wasn't asking a question, but I wanted to say, "Not really. No fun at all."

Rudy walked me back to the front of the bar. "Come on buddy, let me get you in a cab."

I looked around. Stunned. Disoriented. Either this was a dream or everything else was a dream. The choice was mine...

This was real.

I wanted to kiss Rudy, but nobody kissed Rudy. My keys were in my pants. I opened my wallet. My license was where it should be. A picture of me staring back. Me. My name. My address. Even my vitals. The expected was unexpected and exciting.

I reached for a smoke. "My coat, I had a coat." My cigarettes were in the pocket. We looked around for my coat, but couldn't find it anywhere. Rudy sat me on a stool in front of the mural. He told me not to move. He'd see if anyone turned in my jacket.

The mural was behind me. I didn't want to look, but couldn't help myself. There was the sailor lighting his smoke and the leather man with a leg propped against the brick wall, just as I'd remembered. Perfect. Eternal. The third man in the mural was no longer the muscle hunk. Now the third wore a wife-beater and had a thick mustache and sideburns. A denim jacket was tossed at his feet. For years I'd wanted to be that fantasy. Not anymore. The cost was too great.

Rudy returned a moment later and said he couldn't find my coat. I told him I must have left it someplace else.

IDENTITY THEFT

He'd been around for years.

His was the voice whispering in my ear. Telling me things I didn't want to hear. Reminding me of things I had hoped to forget. He fed my paranoia and fears. Undermined my self-esteem. He was so calculating in the ways he stirred me up.

He said I was being talked about and cheated on and stolen from. Trust became impossible after listening to him for a few years. He wanted me to retaliate and stand up for myself. Persuading me into acts of revenge.

He had coaxed that sort of thing since I was a kid and the playground bullies started pushing me and calling me a sissy. "An eye for an eye." I always figured he was born of those schoolyard ruffians, a product of the pain from their fists and shoves. The name calling hurt even more. Some of those wounds still haven't healed. He came to my rescue. He was my anesthesia, my first escape.

I called him Silver for reasons I don't recall. Maybe after the silver of those playground monkey bars or of sunlight reflected on the surrounding cement. Maybe he named himself. The thought was absurd, but I didn't dismiss it. Absurdity is the cornerstone of my story.

Silver taught me to fight and lie and sometimes hide. Oftentimes I was unable to do what needed to be done, so Silver taught me to step aside. When that happened I felt myself flake and crumble away. Silver was what lay beneath. Maybe I named him Silver became he was the lining that stood behind me. Silver was mean and crazy and did things people didn't expect.

He bit and pissed and was apt to use anything as a weapon.

One day Silver went early to school. He went to the playground and greased the money bars with cooking oil. One of his biggest tormentors fell from there that day. He cried like a baby after landing on his shoulder. He was out of school for a week. Another time Silver broke a classmate's knuckle with a pair of pliers. Roger had been tormenting me and Silver finally had enough. Silver said he'd better not squeal. Or else. Silver began to like making others feel fear. Roger told his parents he'd fallen on the ice. Even before high school, the bullies were afraid of me. Or at least of Silver. Everyone was. Silver made good on threats.

My grades in high school were dismal, but I didn't care. My mind was elsewhere. Nowhere really. What I wanted was secondary. Silver had different plans for us. School was boring, a waste of time. Silver didn't take suggestions or entertain other points of view. He knew what he knew and needed nothing more. He had my future planned. College was never an option. By then life was about keeping Silver happy.

I started working the assembly line at Randrow Fixtures less than a week after graduation. Silver opted for a job over a career. Silver's decisions weren't always the wrong ones. The mindless redundancy of factory work appealed to me. Most assemblymen considered the job boring. I saw it as comfortable. Demanding work had no appeal to me. I had enough challenges off the line.

Randrow paid a solid hourly wage with mandatory raises based on time. Paid vacations. All I wanted was my own apartment. After my first two paychecks, I moved out. Mom begged me to stay. Said she didn't want to be alone. I almost laughed. She made that decision a long way back. The night I moved into my furnished studio apartment, she was too drunk to care. Never wanted anything bigger than a studio. I could only be in one room at a time anyway. Been here five years and there's still nothing on my walls. Anything I put up I'd eventually have to take down someday.

Mom's place was always full of crap. Cluttered with reminders of other times and better circumstances. Booze made her blind to the way things were and the things that had taken over her life. Her place was condemned by year's end. No surprise there. I figured that would happen once I wasn't around to put things in the trash and take the garbage outside. I worried people from the city might come looking for me to take her in. They never did. Maybe she said I'd died. Maybe they didn't know about me. Not sure whatever became of her.

I can't go back in time and do things differently. Even if I could, I'd only go back to take more things when I left. More plates and utensils. I should have taken it all. By then Mom wasn't eating anyway.

There was a resale shop on my way to work that I figured would be perfect for kitchen things. I wasn't looking for anything fancy. And this place wasn't that. The resale shop was dim inside and packed to the rafters. The shop smelled of mildew. The guy behind the counter was reading a dog-eared thriller. He smelled like mildew too.

"Plates?" Asking wasn't typically my way, but this place was organized by a logic I didn't understand.

The fellow jerked his head to the side to indicate the smaller room to the side of the counter before tucking some long gray hair behind his ear.

The room featured a cluttered kitchen scene. Plates and silverware, pots and pans, appliances and whatnot were all arranged around a kitchen table with a bowl of plastic as the centerpiece. Aside the stove was a female mannequin in a lopsided wig and an apron. The lady of the house. A mannequin in a business suit was propped on the other side of the room. The husband home from work. Off for work? Although he was painted plaster, he seemed familiar. I recognized the light in those amber plastic eyes. Silver recognized it too.

Silver walked over. He spoke to the mannequin in words I can't remember or a language I didn't understand. The memory is a jumble. I only regained awareness when I felt Silver slip a carving knife in my pocket. I had been saying something. To myself? To the mannequin? I suspected the latter. He looked as though he was turned more my way. Silver and me bought four plates at .25 cents each. Dollar even. No tax. Can't say that I needed four plates. I never had company. Ever.

I never wanted a family or a partner. What was the point? At the end of the day you can't rely on anyone except yourself. I'd had a relationship or two, nothing serious. Silver made sure things didn't go past a certain point. Silver didn't like others getting too close. He's jealous. Possessive of me that way. He claims they upset things, ruin all we have. He liked listing people's faults in my mind, and repeating them. Things would get worse if it was romantic. Silver would keep at it so much that not seeing the guy was the only alternative to going mad... or worse. I'd seen what he was capable of doing.

Silver wanted to go to the resale shop at least once a week. Inevitably we ended up in that room. That mannequin was always the source of attraction and whatever went on between them, Silver kept a secret.

"What are you talking about in there?" the shopkeeper finally said.

130

I told him I was practicing a speech.

"In different voices?"

The comment shook me, but I wasn't about to let this old codger see that. "Just do your job," I said and tossed a hand towel on the counter. That man had never spoken to me before.

"Bye Mr. Silver," he said as we left.

He knew his name.

Next time we went to the resale shop, the front door was padlocked. Silver rattled the chains and the door handle and pounded the glass. The sign said the shop was closed for business. There was nothing inside. Silver was not expecting this. Silver did not like surprises.

Silver knew we should have come last week. On the way home he was smoldering. I was hungry for something to eat. Sometimes a full belly quieted him. Sometimes. We angled the car into a spot in front of a pub that had half pounders. A burger to go sounded good. A man with overgrown sideburns was at the bar with some buddies when I gave the bartender my order. The moment I opened my mouth he began laughing and looking my way. I wasn't sure what that was about, but Silver was in a foul mood and had his suspicions. This guy probably just laughed at the wrong time. I was already falling away when I felt my jaw clench and my fist tighten. Silver muttered that this joker was going to pay. He claimed to be doing this for us, but he was doing it for himself, because he wanted to and because he was in a foul state. Silver didn't do things for others. No reason bigger than himself. When that fellow got up to leave his buddy called out, "Later Crank."

"What kind of asshole over forty goes by the name of Crank?" whispered Silver.

The way he said it, and the way I felt as those words issued from my lips, I shouldn't have been surprised by events to come. I suppose I didn't want to consider it.

We didn't wait for my burger. I slapped a five on the counter and called out that I had to go. We followed Crank outside and around the corner. He had a souped-up Mustang. Figured he'd be driving a ride like that. The engine roared to life. Crank squealed out of there like he was seventeen instead of forty seven. My car was parked a couple of spots away. Silver followed. I remember our eyes in the rearview mirror, and the dividing line racing beneath the front bumper.

We followed Crank for nearly ten miles. He never realized he was being tailed. Eventually he pulled into a three-level parking garage. Silver parked on the street. An aluminum baseball bat was tossed in the yard beside the building. "Meant to be," murmured Silver. He had a convenient take on destiny. I felt his grip on the bat handle and a flash of what was coming. We crept into the garage as the barrier arm descended. The Mustang was just ahead, taking two parking places. Asshole. We ducked behind a cement pillar by the elevator just as Crank got out of the car. We heard his cough as his footsteps approached. Silver came from behind the pillar and brought the bat to Crank's knee. Crack. I heard bone break. Crank collapsed to the pavement.

A moment later, he shouted. "What the fuck man!"

Silver brought the bat down upon the opposite ankle.

Crank howled even more. Silver didn't worry about the noise or witnesses or any of that. He was too busy feeding on pain and fear. Silver took a couple mock swings with the bat and laughed every time Crank flinched. "I'll swing again when you least expect..." Silver brought the bat down upon his shoulder. "...it."

"You're fucking crazy! You're a fucking crazy bastard!"

My lips stretched into a smile. "Yep, and that sucks for you."

Silver waited until Crank crawled to the elevator door and let him inch up the wall to the call buttons before smashing his hand. Crank slid to the ground, leaving a trail of blood along the metal door. Silver was getting bored. At some point this game became too easy for him. Silver hated being bored. He raised the bat and brought it down on Crank's head with a thick sickening thud. Again. Again. At some point the sound at contact changed. Crank no longer seemed human. At some point hitting his skull became like smashing a pumpkin, nothing but pulp and juice.

Then the world went blank.

The aluminum bat hit the cement and rolled to a stop. I was outside the parking garage, sitting at a picnic table beside a laundry tree. Silver had vented, then vanished. He was done. Sated. I was left with blood on my hands and the weapon inches away. I picked up the bat and tried to wipe my prints off the handle. Undoubtedly there were more prints out there. More things implicating me. Had I touched the side of the Mustang or the elevator door? There was no returning to the scene. Too risky. I prayed everything would turn out. With that as my prayer, I had to wonder who was my God?

I moved through the shadows to the car. Once I was at the wheel I tried to calm myself. I didn't know this area of town. After a few minutes I got my bearings and made my way home.

I watched the news the next morning with a knotted stomach. The "mutilated body" (as reported) had been discovered by a nurse coming home from her shift at a nearby hospital. She appeared shaken. Tired. Confused. I felt for her. Nobody needs to happen upon that after a long day at work. The newscaster said there were no leads in the death of the 39 year-old. Crank looked older, even in bar lighting. The investigation continued. Police were questioning neighbors and combing the scene for clues. The statement reignited my fear of prints or surveillance cameras or witnesses or anything else I may have overlooked. The homicide was labelled a random killing. No known motive. Crank's real name was Fenwick. I understood why he went by Crank.

A week passed with no additional leads or news updates. Unsolved and mystery were words soon associated with the murder. After another week I thought that might be the end it. But Silver had other ideas. I should have known better. I knew how he'd felt wielding that bat.

Silver had always enjoyed pain and punishment and control. He'd tasted blood in the past, but he'd never taken a life. After that, all else was a pale imitation. And Silver was never one to deny himself. The lives of those who irritated or threatened him were inconsequential. "I'm only doing what they would do to us if they had the guts." He could justify anything. Silver never wavered once he made up his mind. His word was law. No view existed but his own.

The second time it happened I knew what was coming. Silver was already in control when he took a

134

carving knife from the silverware drawer and wrapped it in a towel. The same knife he's taken from the resale shop. Silver said he'd had enough. "Us or them," he'd said, slipping the blade inside our coat. Enough was an ironic choice of words. Silver never had enough.

Then his hands were on the wheel and his eyes were in the rearview mirror. By the time I knew where we were headed, it was after ten. Tonight was not a good night for going out. I worked early in the morning. Silver didn't care. He preferred me exhausted. Fatigue made me that much easier to control.

Silver parked on a side street near the main gay strip. Numerous muggings had been reported in the area over the past month. The actual number was probably double that. Most gay men aren't too keen on running to the police. Silver went bar to bar, drinking and flashing cash and aping the acts of a much drunker man. "Baiting the catch," was what he had whispered. Explanation was unnecessary. I knew what he was doing.

Walking down a darkened street, I heard someone following me. We knew who it was. Silver and I saw the punk outside the last bar, standing in the shadows, pretending to be on his phone, pretending to be waiting for a ride or a friend. He was waiting all right. Waiting and pretending. His wait was over. As for the pretending, things were about to get real.

The punk pushed himself from the wall a moment after we staggered by. Silver knew he'd follow. He had a sixth sense about those sorts of things. I felt the knife in my coat and felt Silver's smirk. He was eager. Excited. We turned down a dim side street. The punk's footsteps quickened. Boots with a metal heel. Maybe steel toed. Click. Scrape. Narrowing the distance between us. Unknowingly narrowing the distance between himself and the great unknown. I wanted to turn. Call out. I had no mouth to scream. Silver had muted me. He wanted this, and he wanted me as an audience. Near the mouth of an alley, Silver slowed our pace.

His shadow blocked the streetlight behind. He was making his move. When the punk went to grab us, Silver grabbed his hand and in a single movement drew the blade across his wrist. The thin line of red widened. Blood began to drip. Still gripping his hand, Silver turned and drove the blade into the mugger's stomach. Not a fatal stab, a painful and debilitating one. When Silver retracted the blade, dampness spread across the basher's dark t-shirt. His face registered surprise and then panic.

The fun was just beginning. Dying from loss of blood takes time. Silver slashed one cheek, then moved the blade across the punk's forehead. Blood ran into his eyes and dripped from his jaw. He held his belly with a reddening hand.

Silver drew the punk closer. He held him from behind. His hands encircled his waist as he whispered, "Yes." Silver knew what that the punk was thinking. "But not just yet." The sidewalk was slick with blood.

The punk's legs buckled as Silver dragged him behind a hedge. The shadowed row of bushes would suit his purposes. Silver brought the blade to his lips and licked the edge clean. He lowered the knife. The basher's eyes were wide. Silver laughed, "Don't scream, or make a sound, or I'll slit your throat now." He grabbed the punk by the hair and held his head steady. "Shhhh." Silver guided the blade into the anterior of the mugger's neck. "I always wanted to perform a tracheotomy." Blood oozed around the tip of the blade. Now there's be no screaming. Given his injuries, he would either bleed to death or choke on his own blood. Either one would suffice. The slow seepage of life offered ample time for reflection. Silver sat on the ground and tossed bits of grass upon the punk's chest. The kid was struggling for breath. Struggling to stay alive. We sat for ten minutes and watched the life drain and his eyes cloud. We listened for the breath of life to escape. Supposedly the soul resides in that exhalation. That's what Mom told me. She said she saw her mother's soul leave the earth and that it looked like cinnamon colored smoke. When I asked if she knew my soul's color she looked into my eyes a moment and said, "That's a secret best kept until the day that you die."

When the punk breathed his last we strained to see in the darkness, but saw no soul mingled with his breath of life. Maybe because I was looking through Silver's eyes. Maybe having a soul is a requirement for seeing one. His open eyes gazed into forever. Silver kissed his lifeless lips. In movies they close a dead person's eyes. Silver left them open.

Those eyes were the last thing I remember. When I came to it was 2:45 and I was in my kitchen. Silver was suddenly gone and I was spreading peanut butter on toast with the murder weapon. Dried blood still crusted the handle. Two hours had passed since we left the bar. Ninety minutes since I'd lost consciousness. Getting home probably took a half hour which left a full hour missing. Had I sat with the punk all that time? Had I gone back for seconds? I should have cared more than I did.

No clues in the second homicide either. No fingerprints. No skin beneath his nails. No neighbors were watching from darkened windows. No suspicious bartender. Nothing. Silver was either a genius, or charmed, or an invisible man. But someday things wouldn't go so smoothly. Someday there'd be a mistake. A witness. A fingerprint. A survivor. An arrest. The thought of Silver killing was terrible, but the thought of getting caught was even worse. The bloodletting would continue. Silver would never stop after tasting the power of life and death. If anything, the killing would escalate.

This couldn't continue, but I had no idea how to stop it.

If killing excited him, maybe I needed to make my life more exciting. My life had been routine, but stringing habit after habit calmed me. That was the way I'd lived. Silver had wanted that at one time, too. He was the main reason things were as they were. But he'd changed since the resale shop. Maybe that mannequin had whispered something to him. Perhaps those perfectly painted lips had sown discontent. Now Silver wanted thrills and adventure. Now he liked taking risks.

The next day at work I went to Dick in Human Resources and put in for a ten day vacation. I had time coming. I had a right to ask. I hadn't taken one day in five years. Not even a sick day. Not the day I moved and not the day(s) after I'd killed. That says something about my work ethic.

The thought of taking time and going someplace made my hands and voice tremble. Dick gave me a queer look when he shook my hand. I reminded him of my name. I'd never been to see him before. He whistled through his teeth when he retrieved my file. Randrow employees with perfect attendance were rare. "Never left early. Never even been late." HR was uneasy with that sort of record. Dick eagerly gave me the time.

I told my crew boss I'd be gone the next two weeks. Family emergency. I'd be out of town. People at work missed all the time because of family. Sick children. Aging parents. Wives giving birth. Weddings. Funerals. The word family always worked. My crew boss said, "No problem."

Later he said he hoped everything was okay and that he didn't realize I had a family. Why would he know? He knew nothing about me. I'd made sure that none of them did.

For all practical purposes, I didn't have a family. My people were dead. Mom might still be alive, but everything was dead to her except the bottle. Mom was big on promising to change. That was as far as it went. I got tired of throwing coins in an empty well.

I claimed I wanted a change of scenery, but Silver wasn't fooled. He knew what I really needed was a vacation from the stress and fear. He knew his killing bothered me, but he didn't care. My anxiety only increased his pleasure in taking lives.

After arranging the time off, I still needed to decide where to go. There were plenty of options. I stopped at the travel agency I passed each day on my way to work. A faded cardboard palm tree leaned against the front window. Beside it was a poster of a beach with the word "Aloha" written across sand and surf. Bells announced my entry. Inside a small dog was curled on a pillow. I didn't recognize the breed. I'm not a dog person. The scent of sandalwood hung in the air. A shelving unit along one wall held dozens of brochures. While looking through them I picked up several with appealing cover photos. The travel agent introduced herself as June. "Looks like you're exploring possibilities. Fun isn't it?"

I admitted I'd never travelled much before. June assured me I'd love it. "People always do." She suggested a guided tour. "More direction for the novice traveler." June asked if I was traveling with a friend or companion. I told her no. She said traveling alone was all the more reason to go with a group. I said I wasn't looking to meet people. Unfazed, June asked when I was leaving. When I told her, she said arranging something for next week wouldn't be a problem. "Sometimes you can save a bundle with last minute bookings. Let's take a look at some possibilities."

June knew how to sell a vacation. Twenty minutes later I was booked on a seven day cruise in the Western Caribbean. I hoped the sea and the sun would bring some relief. The ship departed from Houston with stops in Cozumel, Costa Maya, and Grand Cayman. There were other places I can't recall. I'd heard about the doings on those grand cruise ships. Coworkers had been on them.

June said the demographic on cruise ships tends to skew a little old. "Lots of empty nesters. Recent retirees." I told her I didn't mind, as long as everything was included. Meals, excursions, tips, etc. She said it was. When I asked about privacy, June said that nowadays being aboard a luxury liner was like staying in a hotel at sea. She said a fellow could be the life of the ship, reclusive, or anything in between. "Whatever you choose." I liked having the option.

A week later I was off. The trip to Houston was my first plane ride ever. Flying didn't bother me. I wasn't a fan of the crowding on the jet, but I liked the thought of moving through space at incredible speeds. Closing my eyes, I could hear the whistle and feel the rush of that momentum. I couldn't predict the future, but I liked the notion of traveling more. Some folks at work took trips twice a year. That could be me. With no kids or family to consider, money wasn't an issue. My issue was Silver.

My plane landed ten minutes early at George Bush Intercontinental, and then took twenty minutes to taxi to the gate. I collected my suitcase. Outside the cab driver popped the trunk and put my baggage inside. I'd heard cab drivers don't always know English so I pressed the address of the hotel against the plastic divider. When he tried to talking to me, I pretended not to understand. Houston is vertical and modern, steel and glass. Sun and sky were reflected everywhere. The taxi rounded the drive to the front door of the fancy hotel June had booked for me. She finagled a suite on the 37th floor. The hotel was convenient to the Port of Houston. I was due at the ship after 9:00 tomorrow morning for an 11:00 departure.

My room was fancy! The only other hotel rooms I'd been in were at the Cozy Inn back home where I'd gone with a couple of hooked-ups. That was sure nothing like being here. This place was double the size of my studio apartment. The bed was as big as a bus. The balcony took my breath away. Even birds were below me. Once I got acclimated, I got a beer from the minibar and sat taking in the view. I closed my eyes and felt the sun on my face. The moment made me realize how small my life had become. I'd seen so little of the world. This was my first time out of my home state. Seeing new things got me excited about the future. I was still young, but Silver made me feel much older. Sometimes I felt like instead of being in my twenties I was twice that. Maybe I was our ages combined.

Next morning I awoke to screaming. I wrestled myself from a vague and nameless dream. I took a moment to recognize the room. The screaming was the

141

gulls. The light outer curtain billowed in the morning breeze. The door to the balcony was open. I thought I'd closed it. Maybe not. I fell back upon the bedding. When you're used to sleeping on a twin mattress, it felt great to roll and stretch and feel nothing but bed. Lying still, I could feel the mattress molding around me, soft and thick as a marshmallow. I never understood how people could stay in bed all day. Now I did. If I didn't have to get moving, I could have dozed for another hour or so.

After showering I collected my things and went to the lobby for breakfast. The hotel set a free spread for guests. There was enough to feed an army and I wasn't shy about getting seconds. By the time I finished breakfast and checked out it was 8:30. The doorman got me a cab to the docks. The harbor was under five minutes away. First time I saw the ship, it took my breath away. The pictures didn't give a real sense of it. I expected big, but this was enormous. I wondered how it even floated.

Checking in was like being at the hotel all over again with lots of bustling going on with greeters, guests, ship staff, porters, and assorted others. My room was two floors down, Stateroom 426. Ocean view with verandah. The desk personnel gave me a copy of the ship's floor plan, circled Stateroom 426, and asked if I needed help with my luggage. I was fine with it. Some people had half a dozen trunks and suitcases.

"If you need anything else, or if we can be of service in any way, please just let us know."

I nodded.

"We hope you enjoy sailing with us," she added, moving on to the next guest.

Stateroom 426 was a good deal smaller than my room last night, but still more than I expected. There was a queen sized bed and a nightstand, a chest of drawers, a writing desk, a convertible sofa with end table, a dining table with two chairs, and a bathroom with tub and rain shower. On the far wall was a glass door and a verandah above the water. After putting away my things, I picked up a folder on the table and leafed through it. Inside were the menus for meals during the cruise, a list of activities, another map of the ship, and pamphlets and information about each of the islands we were visiting. This was already an adventure.

Curious about the rest of the ship, I decided to go exploring. I'd never seen anything like this. Endless corridors of rooms. Things I didn't expect: gift shops and boutiques, fountains and a garden. A barber shop and a beauty shop. A gym. A movie theater. A cabaret and a dinner theater. Bars. Lounges. A disco. Coffee shop. Dining room. Casino. Indoor and two outdoor swimming pools. Whirlpool. Shuffle board court. Skeet shooting. Tourist information center and more things I can't recall. Most places were open around the clock. My coworkers at Randrow were right about one thing, these cruise ships were unbelievable.

The people streaming on board seemed from every walk of life. Older married couples. Several children. Honeymooners. Lesbian and gay couples. A group of girlfriends whose overloud conversation revealed they'd gone to college together. I was an anomaly which was fine by me. I liked my privacy and the option of keeping a distance. Being alone in a place like this was synonymous with being invisible.

On my second spin around the deck I spied him. Looking to the Gulf beyond the harbor. Handsome profile. Tall with reddish brown hair. A bit husky, not sporting the lean brand of physique that's so in fashion.

He was alone. Mid-thirties. Strong jaw. Forceful chin. Full lips. His serious expression was intriguing. Brooding. Melancholy. I wondered if it was who he was or if it was there for a reason.

I took a place at the railing several feet away. I was conscious of not wanting to intrude, but unable to keep walking. The attraction was powerful. He seemed familiar. After a bit he wiped his eyes and walked away, never glancing in my direction. Had he been crying or were his eyes irritated by the sea breeze? I followed him down the deck before he turned to take a stairwell. Eventually I lost sight of him amidst the flurry of bodies and activity below deck. I was frustrated, but figured that over the course of the next seven days I was bound to see him again. Maybe then I would understand the attraction. The stranger was reason enough not to be a hermit on the cruise.

Before dinner that evening I went to one of the bars for a cocktail. Making conversation with a table of strangers would require liquid courage. I was about to order a beer when I felt myself fade. Silver called for a Manhattan. He was bored already. He wondered what I'd hoped to gain by taking a cruise. He was teasing. If Silver was vehemently opposed, we wouldn't be here. Before I was halfway through my drink, the man I'd seen earlier sat down two stools away. Vodka tonic. Alone. He caught Silver's eye a couple times in the mirror behind the bar. Was he bored? Curious? Cruising while cruising? The third time we traded glances, Silver raised a glass to him. He echoed the gesture and smiled.

His smile was nice.

When Silver ordered another Manhattan, he bought the stranger another Vodka Tonic. Silver could be so direct. My discomfort amused him. He said I couldn't wait for what I wanted. I had to take it. When the bartender placed a cocktail before him, the man slid to the stool beside me. Silver was gone.

In a Texas accent, he introduced himself as Clive. I liked the way he spoke. We shook hands. "Thanks for the drink." He nodded towards the glass. "Just what the doctor ordered." Clive must have seen my confusion. "Alcohol, it's a magic elixir for the newly divorced." He already had a couple cocktails beneath his belt.

That explained his melancholia. "I'm sorry, how long were you married to her..."

"Him," Clive corrected. "I was married to him." His eyes began to moisten. "Not long. Not even a year. Barely nine months, but I loved him."

I looked down at my drink. Despite my efforts, no nugget of wisdom or comfort came to mind. Awkward moments like this were one reason I was never a fan of conversation. I hated not knowing the right thing to say. "I guess length isn't the best way to measure it."

"I've always been more a fan of girth," he winked.

I must have blushed because Clive apologized. With a slap on the back he admitted he was a bit tipsy. He said that once he had one too many, there was no filter on what came out of his mouth. "Besides, I plan on enjoying being unattached for a while ... playing the field. Know what I mean? I didn't come on this cruise looking for anything. Nothing serious anyway."

I was unsure of what I said, but he replied with, "You've got that right. I didn't book this vacation for a trip on The Love Boat." Clive ran a hand through his hair and added something beneath his breath. "See what I mean about running off at the mouth. Sometimes all a body needs to do is say Hello and they get my life story."

"That's not so bad."

Clive tipped his drink my direction. "A true martyr. You seem like a nice guy."

"I can be."

His stool swiveled my way. "Nice and easy to talk to. Young. Easy on the eyes. You've probably got a boyfriend. Was that him earlier?"

Clive had a clumsy way of asking if I was single. "I don't have a boyfriend."

He put a hand on my shoulder and leaned close. "Did you already hook up with that guy?"

I had no idea what he was talking about. "Who?"

Clive lowered his voice. "That guy you were talking to a minute ago."

I was still blank.

"The man sitting here before I slid over. I thought you were with him. You seemed like a couple, or at least you seemed together." A moment later he added. "Oh shit, are you two brothers? You kind of look alike."

Was I that drunk or was Clive seeing double? Maybe he was nuts. I had no idea what he was talking about. No one was on that stool. Every stool at the bar was empty except for us. "I don't know who you mean. No one was with me."

"Have it your way."

Maybe Clive just had an odd sense of humor. His hand went from my shoulder to my thigh. The warmth and weight of it made me nervous, excited. The promise it held made my breath shallow. Attraction. Closeness. Intimacy. Sex. Clive nodded towards the mirror. "The guy I thought you were with is by himself over in the third booth."

"Who?"

"Can't miss him. He's looking right at us, and he doesn't look happy. That's why I thought you two were together."

No one was in the third booth. The mirror reflected only us, the bartender, and an elderly couple in the corner booth.

When I asked what he looked like Clive asked if I was messing with him. "Is this some sort of game?" I was about to ask him the same thing when he leaned closer, "You giving me a sobriety test?"

I shook my head no.

Clive said he'd play along. "The guy looks a bit like you. Leaner maybe. Rougher looking. Black clothes. Dark eyes and hair. Thicker brows. Sexy twist of his lips." He was describing Silver as I'd seen him, reflected in mirrors and lurking in dreams, ready to kill or drenched in blood. Tense. Coiled. Wild. Clive's hand moved higher on my thigh. He probably thought my shudder was the result of his touch.

Clive nodded to the bartender and charged the tab to his room. He asked if I'd like to see his cabin. "There's a nice view below." His hand moved higher. "What do you say?"

I was about to take a rain check when the next thing I knew we were walking down the hallway towards his cabin. The ship's passageway appeared foggy. My vision was haloed at the edges. Clive had a hand at my waist, but no one we passed seemed to notice or care.

Clive's grip tightened. "Down this hall a bit further."

I was moving in a haze. We were going to do this. I couldn't back out now even if I wanted to. This was what I'd wanted all along. The rain check seemed

147

like something I should do. Silver had commandeered the moment. Sometimes he was looking out for me.

Clive slid his key card in the door and pushed it open. Inside it smelled like the sea. He flipped on the light. His cabin was considerably smaller than mine. No table and chairs. No sofa bed. No verandah. Just a desk. A bed. A dresser. And a bathroom. The porthole was open. Beyond was nothing but the Gulf and the sound of the ship cutting through the water.

Clive tossed his sweater on the bed. "That's where the magic happens," he laughed. He began to unbutton his shirt and asked if I wanted another drink.

I wasn't sure I could do this.

His chest was broad. Furry.

I could do this.

"Drink?" he repeated.

Before I could answer, I was gone again, sucked into a void without color or sound, nothing to mark the passage of time. Silver liked me present when he killed or was cruel. Otherwise he locked me in that place that was no place. Sometimes he locked me there to deny me pleasure.

Lost time was nothing new. Blackouts had always been part of my life. By the time I realized it was abnormal, it had been happening for years. By then, I knew those episodes were wrong and best kept secret. Being different was undesirable. If Mom or school sent me someplace, they might discover my secrets. Then there'd be repercussions. Consequences. Change. By then Silver was a part of me. By then I'd become adept at concocting excuses and covering lapses. Sometimes the void lasted seconds. Sometimes hours. Every couple months, I lost days. I missed my high school graduation and my father's funeral.

148

For years I didn't know Silver was independent. I thought my episodes were akin to sleepwalking, but I was wrong. Gradually, I became aware of things that Silver had done and things he'd said. Disturbing things. Things hinting that another life was being lived. Silver was a being with his own awareness and agenda, but not his own body. I was unable to keep secrets from him, yet he kept so much from me. Discovering what he'd done after the fact was disturbing. That sort of knowledge wasn't power, it was ridicule.

And Silver seemed to be growing stronger.

And as abruptly as I was gone, I returned. I was staring at the ceiling above Clive's bed. Clive was holding me in his arms. We were naked beneath the covers and in the midst of afterglow. The scent of sex hung in the air. I could taste Clive in my mouth. Condom wrappers were on the nightstand. Thank God.

Clive said he'd never met anyone like me. "You're a mystery." He kissed me. "I'd like to see more of you, a lot more of you, Silver." The moment he said it, Silver's laugh echoed in my head. To my knowledge, he'd never given his name to anyone before. What else had he shared? Clive's arms became as tight and suffocating as tentacles. The room was stifling. Panic consumed me. I needed to get out. I needed to breathe. I said I had to go to my cabin and take care of some things.

"You sure you don't have a boyfriend stashed away?"

I feigned a laugh. The joke was stale. "No, I'm single."

"Young, handsome, voracious, single. What are you hiding?"

If he only knew.

Clive asked if we were still on for a nightcap at midnight. "Don't break my heart by canceling." He said it playfully, but there was more. A fragile desperation. I recalled his recent break-up. I couldn't cancel if I wanted to. Silver was calling the shots. The bedside clock read 10:30. I'd missed four hours. By the rumbling of my stomach I could tell we hadn't eaten. We'd missed both dinner seatings.

I said I'd be there. We agreed to meet at the Castaway Lounge in an hour and a half.

"Then maybe we can come back here again?" he added with a smile.

"Maybe."

As I dressed, Clive propped himself on an elbow, watching me with a certain look in his eyes. Whatever Silver did must have been impressive.

"Remember what we talked about earlier."

I nodded, despite being in the dark. By Clive's tone, I wondered if Silver had made some romantic declaration. If so, what was in it for him? Silver's motives were guided by a thirst for cruelty and power. He didn't feel love or tenderness or compassion. Those soft emotions were the dark side of the moon. But he could mimic them. This romance on the high seas scenario was malarky. Silver cared for no one but himself. Not even me. Especially me.

Clive puckered his lips. "Give me one more."

I kissed him goodbye.

He grabbed my hand, "See you at midnight."

"I'll be there." I wriggled my hand free and hoped it hadn't been too abrupt.

En route to my cabin I felt my heart throbbing in my ears. The sense of dread was undeniable. This was building to something. I suspected Clive was in danger.

Perspiration lined my brow. If I knew what had been promised, I might discover what Silver had in mind. Maybe I could do something to alter the course of events. Vigilance was required for Clive's sake as well as my own.

I peeled out of my clothes and showered. Soaping myself, I discovered scratches and hand prints and the beginnings of a bruise on my thigh. Apparently sex had been intense.

Rather than invigorating, the shower made me feel heavy and fatigued. Exhaustion was an enemy. Exhaustion offered an easy doorway for Silver. I made a quick cup of instant coffee. Another. The caffeine had minimal effect aside from upsetting my stomach. I was certain Silver was aware of my intent and I'm sure it amused him. 11:30. No time for anything but dread.

At midnight I met Clive in the lounge. He was at the bar when I arrived with an empty glass before him and a fresh vodka and tonic beside it. The Castaway Lounge was crowded. Couples. Boozy. Romantic. Dim multi-colored lights to highlight an island motif. The reggae/calypso mix was considerably louder than earlier in the day. I sat beside Clive who leaned close. "Hi-ho Silver," he said, as though it was extremely clever.

Clive patted the stool beside him and whispered, "I've missed you." His eyes revealed deeper feelings. I needed to remain aloof, keep a distance, and damper the longing he felt. Clive tilted his class, "I'm already two ahead of you." He caught the bartender's attention and ordered me a Manhattan.

By the time I took a sip of the cocktail, the hand on that drink was no longer my own. The warm rush of alcohol moved to my belly as Silver swiveled to face Clive. Silver did not dismiss me this time. He wanted me watching from the wings, a mute witness to events unfolding. Silver wanted me to know. He said, "I'm in the mood to walk a bit."

Clive nodded. By then he'd follow Silver anywhere.

"After a walk around deck we can head back to your cabin." As the words escaped my lips, my suspicions were confirmed. Clive was in danger. Silver did not make suggestions without a plan and his plans were typically sick. Silver wanted me to witness all this. My suffering spiked his pleasure and made his cruelty even sweeter. "A quick walk around the ship and back to your cabin," Silver repeated.

Clive downed his vodka and tonic. "Sounds good, though I can take or leave the lap around deck."

Now it was Silver's turn to put a hand on Clive's thigh. Confident. Promising. Clive was under his spell. That touch could convince him of anything. "The fresh air will do us both some good."

Clive once more signed for the drinks. He was tipsy. I worried at first that Silver had drugged him, but then Clive revealed he'd been at the bar since 11:00. "I was eager to see you again. I think you put a spell on me."

Silver rose from the stool. "Magic would take all the fun out of it."

Clive had no idea what he was talking about.

On deck the wind from the Gulf was refreshing. The stars and moon were bright above. After rounding the deck, Silver tightened his grip on Clive's hand and pulled him aside. "Romantic, isn't it?"

Clive nodded.

With a deep kiss, Silver backed Clive into the small outlet of the deck used for skeet shooting during the day. Silver kissed him aggressively, moving down his neck as he pushed Clive against the rail. His fingers worked the buttons on Clive's shirt. Two open. Three. Silver caught a nipple in his teeth and grinding his hips against Clive, pushing him harder against the railing, making him lean further over the edge. Clive was drunk, unsure of his footing. He tried to return Silver's passion, but his hands were clumsy. He was capable of little more than moans. Silver turned him around. Clive was laughing. Obedient. Oblivious. In that moment I knew what was coming. Silver reached for Clive's belt, not to loosen it but to hoist him. Silver's excitement was building. Clive was unaware or maybe life had taken him beyond caring.

I was the only one with a chance of stopping this. The lunacy had to end. The killing had gone on too long. I should have stopped him earlier, but I was afraid. I hoped it would somehow end of its own accord. Now I knew it never would. Clive would not be another of his victims. He'd done nothing but display his weakness and vulnerability. If I let this happen I couldn't live with myself. That seemed the solution either way.

Summoning my reserves of strength, I felt a power begin to rise like a geyser from the depths of our shared form. I knew my capability was a surge, a brief flash. Speed was crucial. Sensation returned to my arms and legs. The nerves were awakened. Fuzziness cleared. Silver was no longer in control. I'd taken him by surprise. Silver would return enraged. Violent. Vengeful. His retaliation would be brutal. Already he was fighting to return.

Not yet. With all my strength I shoved him further inside. There was only one person capable of stopping Silver and only one way to do it. I pushed Clive aside and raised a foot to the railing. The lowest rung was slippery and wet. Eyes forward. Intent clear. The water was dark around me. Only the crests of waves glistened in moonlight. Looking down I saw the white of the wake where the ship churned the waters. We were miles from land.

My foot moved to the second rung. I heard Clive call "Wait," as I straddled the top rail. Was that Clive or Silver? So many voices with just one way to silence them. The voices. The wind. A wail. A plea. A siren's song. My hands gripped the rail. A brief hesitation. Silver would return in seconds. All I needed to do was let go.

I closed my eyes and let it happen. Letting go was easy. No more than not holding on, to anything.

Relax.

Release.

Time so slow as I fell through the dark and into the froth and foam. A insignificant splash. Submerged in the churn. Spun and turned in a bracing medley of bubbles, tossed into a celebratory glass of champagne. Eyes heavenward as I gasped for air. Stars. Moon. Different from here. Fear was blended with victory. I'd conquered him. Silver would join me here. Swallowed by something bigger. We'd lie together at the bottom of the sea. Salt stung my eyes. Away from the undertow of the departing ship. Two figures standing along the back rail. The sight was sharper than could be explained. Clive was there. The figure beside him draped an arm across his shoulder. Silver. They stood watching. Cohorts. Companions.

Clive kissed him. His voice should have been swallowed by the ship and the wind and the waves, but I heard him so clearly. "Now we'll be together, always."

Silver's voice echoed in my head. Amused. "Did you imagine you could best me?" He was laughing. "You've been an oaf since conception. I was here before you and will continue after you're fish food. Your desperation didn't create me. Your desperation was an invitation I accepted. You were a passable host, but you eventually limited and bored me. Your life offered nothing but a desire to move on to something better, to someone more deserving." His arm was around Clive.

"Recognize him?"

Familiar, but distant. Where? Suddenly I saw his resemblance to the resale mannequin, but slightly different.

"He became flesh as well."

And then I realized the difference and knew what had been happening all along. The mannequin needed a vessel, something to house whatever he was. The murders were a means to an end. The flesh of Crank and pieces of the hoodlum punk comprised the substance of Clive. He was the product of their flesh. A patchwork without stitching.

The cruise to get away from it all had been their plan. A ploy. Our chance meeting. Clive's story and divorce and my need to protect him had all been orchestrated and undoubtedly a source of ongoing amusement. Silver did nothing by chance. I should have known. Making me part of my own undoing only fed his ego.

"We're quite a team. Thank you for jumping and saving us the trouble." Silver and Clive gave a playful goodbye salute from the back of the deck and as they did, the border between them blurred and they melded into one. "Togetherness," was the last word I heard him say.

I turned in a circle.

Silence.

Silver was gone and I was alone. For the first time since those schoolyard days I was truly on my own. The Gulf was vast. Water. Sky. Horizon. A world of such simple components. Salty waves lapped over me. Stinging. Crusting in my hair and ears. I felt the great dark depths ready to pull me down a final time. The sea had nothing but time.

I slipped off my pants and tied a knot in either leg. I swung them over my head to capture some air as a float. The effect was brief. I had a hole in a back pocket. Not large, but large enough. I attempted again and tried to hold my hand over the hole. By then my pants were soaked and the effort was pointless.

Eventually exhaustion would overcome me and I'd be pulled down as I had been so many times with Silver. But this time he wouldn't be my conqueror.

I began to shout until I got a mouthful of salt. There was no one to hear my cries. The ship was already some distance away, little more than a shadow on the horizon. Once more I spit out water from the waves washing over me. I tried floating on my back, looking up at the stars. Brilliant. Beautiful. Vast. I wondered what color my soul might be and if I still possessed one after all that occurred.

I've heard it said that once the struggling ends, drowning is a peaceful way to die. Peace sounded so welcome.

THE RETURN

He first came to me on the evening of May 3rd. That dark anniversary. The day had been exhausting. Five minutes after hitting the sheets, I was asleep. As the dream began, I was walking down a relatively deserted street in an industrial section of a city. The cracked sidewalk buckled and erupted with bursts of weeds. Most of the buildings were boarded or deserted. Planks over the windows were riddled with graffiti. The day was overcast and yet this world was bathed in a strange golden glow. The air was thick. There was the sound of the wind and little else.

A man was walking down the sidewalk towards me. Tall. Shirtless. Moving with a swagger that came from knowing himself and these streets. A dirty white t-shirt was tucked in the waist of his low slung jeans. A serpent tattoo wrapped around one shoulder, curling down his lean torso and disappearing below the elastic band of his underwear. He looked side to side as he approached. Then he looked straight ahead. He caught my eye and sneered.

His hair was buzzed beneath his angled ball cap. He looked to be a bad boy, a tasty piece of rough trade. My cock twitched. The night visitor read the lust in my eyes. He knew the score. Reading lust in men's eyes was nothing new to him. Less than half a block remained between us. Looking me in the eye once more, he gave me a nervy smile that promised more. For a price.

I turned to see a utility van rumble by. Plain white with a side ladder. Screeching to a stop, it backed into the alley between me and the tattooed man. The driver checked his side mirrors for clearance. A

157

newspaper blew down the street and wrapped around my feet. The headline and the picture below it looked familiar, but the wind swept the paper into the air and it vanished. I heard the beeping of the vehicle in reverse. The sound grew louder.

More insistent.

Disturbing.

I opened my eyes. The beeping van transformed into the alarm on my cell phone.

Morning already? My sleep medication affected me that way sometimes, yet last night was the opposite of the typical blankness. The dream had been vivid and sensual. Full of details. I still could see the handsome face, chiseled torso, and assertive stride of the man on the sidewalk. Familiar. The image remained as I made my morning coffee. I masturbated in the shower to the memory.

My day was filled with distractions. The scene of my dream and the night visitor were buried in the debris of routine by noon.

Two nights later, the dream returned. Same sidewalk. Same shirtless man. This time I noticed his thin sculpted beard and how it highlighted his jawline. I saw the sunglasses hooked in the front pocket of his jeans and his heavy work boots. The same truck backed into the alley. This time I didn't hear it beep as it reversed slowly between the buildings. Once it cleared I again had an unobstructed view of the man.

He was leaning against a red brick building, having a smoke. Arms at his side. Crotch pushed forward. One hand lingering near. He was making himself available. Watching. As I walked by I could smell his sweat mixed with cigarette smoke. Dark brown eyes followed me. He said something I didn't understand, but the meaning was clear. I stopped farther up the block and sat on some stone steps. I looked down and waited. A moment later a pair of work boots stepped into view. No surprise. I raised my eyes to appraise the worn jeans, the promising crotch, the lean, tattooed torso, and, finally, his face. The night visitor wore the same cocky smirk. This was a transaction, but money wasn't an issue. Sex was the issue. Money was a means to an end. A stake in the game. I pulled a couple twenties from my pocket. The man flicked his cigarette and pocketed the bills. He nodded towards an abandoned building across the street. I asked his name. "Call me Vic," he answered without looking. He didn't ask for mine, but John would do.

Then we were beside a large bed. Mattress worn and stained. The room was sweltering and covered with dirt and dust. On my knees on the filthy floor. Vic stood with his arms behind his head, allowing himself to be serviced. Nothing more. "You enjoy me a little more this time, huh?" he said. I didn't understand, but didn't care. The fat piece making me gag was all I cared about.

Vic began to face fuck me more aggressively. He was used to being worshipped. Used to johns paying the price to serve him. That tool deserved to be worshipped. Large. Uncut. Thick. His prick had probably pleased a lot of women. He was a stud, capable of getting some whenever and wherever he wanted. Fucking was probably his favorite pastime.

I looked up from my kneeling position. Vic's eyes were closed. Every muscle on his lean body was tightening and rising through his skin, defined by a sheen of sweat. He was getting close. I wanted to prolong things, but knew Vic would only tolerate this for so long. This was business. Time was money. My prick was straining against the fabric of my work pants. Denying myself release added to the moment.

The night visitor's breath quickened. His hands moved from behind his head to the side of my head. He wrapped my hair in his fingers and pulled my mouth forward. I felt that unmistakable throb and expansion. A moment later Vic moaned and buried himself deep in my throat. I didn't understand what he said, but the meaning was clear. Then, deflating. I let his prick fall from my lips, enormous in its softened but still swollen state. Vic pulled up his jeans and tucked himself inside. With a nod, he left the room. Sunlight burst through the clouds and illuminated the filth streaked window. Dust motes moved in the shafts of light. Floorboards creaked, expanding with the heat. The sound transformed into footfalls above. With each step, a puff of dust billowed from the ceiling.

I awoke sweating. Sunlight was on my back and I was painfully aroused. I flipped over and recalled as much of the dream as he could. The feel of the floor beneath my knees. The taste of that fat, uncut prick. The fullness of Vic's balls and the tang of his load. I heard his mystery words of ecstasy. Romanian. Greek. Memories so vivid than in moments I dug my heels into the mattress and felt the rise of release. Only when my breathing calmed did I realize that I'd been shouting. I was unsure what to make of all this. I couldn't recall ever having a recurring dream, but I was eager to have it again.

Two nights later, the dream expanded. Everything was identical, but with greater elaboration. Gaps filled. When Vic nodded towards the abandoned building, I rose. As we crossed the street, a woman layered in filthy clothes was rocking on an orange plastic

160

milk crate in the vacant lot. Paper and plastic danced about her in the gusting wind. In the dance I saw the familiar newspaper headline, but still couldn't discern the accompanying picture or words.

A storm front was moving in. Periodically, the woman shouted. Her words were gibberish or perhaps only lost in the howl of wind or the coo of pigeons from the eaves. I hadn't noticed the birds before, lining every inch of rain gutter. Hundreds. Thousands.

As I entered with building with Vic, the woman shouted, "That place." There was more, but that was all I could understand until a moment later when she added, "Not what it seems, the inside has come outside." When we stepped across the threshold, I saw what she meant. The building only extended twenty feet beyond the facade. The back portion was open. Mostly demolished. Beyond was overgrown rubble of brick and glass. Some weeds were several feet high. The coo of the pigeons was deafening.

Vic snapped his finger for my attention. No humor marked his face. Trade had no time for that. Vic led me up a staircase on the front part of the structure. He warned me to watch my step. The stairs creaked at every footfall. One wall of the staircase had fallen away. The plaster lay below upon a pile of bricks, exposing a twisted skeleton of reinforcement wire. On the landing above were two doors. Vic opened the first.

I remembered the room. The narrow bed. The broken chair. The size and decor made me think this was an old hotel or flophouse. Vic closed the door behind him, testing the wall before leaning against it. He unzipped. I knelt on the wooden plank floor. Afterwards, Vic zipped his jeans and left.

Sun shone through the filthy windowpane. I wanted fresh air, but the window had warped from its track. As I lay on the bed, the springs squeaked and the mattress bowed. I expected it to smell worse than it did. The sun felt good on my body. I rubbed my belly and thought of Vic.

Then I was in a dream within a dream. Different, but still familiar. I was in another hotel, navigating winding and shadowed corridors tinged with red. Men roamed the hallways there, searching. I felt my heart beat harder as I moved through the crowd. I was in pursuit. I caught glimpses of my quarry's muscled form just ahead, rounding a corner or going through a door. Out of earshot. Out of reach. I had to reach him. I had to...

There was a thud and the creak of footfalls from above. I was back on the bed in the abandoned room. There was a flash. A clap of thunder. The homeless woman across the alley was screaming. Papers and leaves and rubbish blew down the sidewalk on either side of her. At the next flash of lightning, she rushed around the corner. When she disappeared, the torrent began. Rain pounded on the roof. The room would be my refuge until there was a break in the rain. I had nowhere else to go. I was an alien in this world.

Someone was descending the stairs, and pausing outside my closed door. I was unsure of what to expect or of who else might be living here. The moment of anticipation stretched. Nothing. Had I imagined the footfalls, or had the unknown person moved on? The room had changed. The chair was gone as was the standing lamp in the corner. I wondered if those things had been removed while I was asleep.

Drops rolled across the cracked ceiling plaster and collected near the light fixture before dropping to the floor. A small puddle had already formed there, muddying a spot on the dusty floorboards. Drops continued to plop into the widening pool.

When I opened my eyes again, I was back in my own bed. The drip drip drip of the dream became the drip of the kitchen faucet. Water had collected in the pot I'd used for popcorn last night. I wondered what the dream meant. Recurring dreams had to have a significance. My upstairs neighbor was getting his things together. He always went to the gym before work. Maybe those had been the footfalls in my dream. Much could be explained, but that didn't mean it made sense.

Looking at clock I realized I'd overslept. Toughest part of my barista job was the early morning wake-up when I was scheduled to open. I jumped in the shower and was at the Bean Factory by six. Stu, the assistant manager, was already inside. Stu was a musician who did this as his day job. Stu understood the oversleeping thing. Sometimes he arrived directly from a gig. Stu had the proper perspective on this job. The Bean Factory was his paycheck, not his dream. Getting here on time was preferable, but not a life or death situation. Stu understood this was all temporary.

I threw my backpack behind the counter.

Stu hired me when I moved to town six months ago. At the time, I needed to leave St. Louis for my survival. That town held too many memories and too much Andrew for a new start. In November, I came to town for a long weekend. The change of scenery felt good. I went home, collected my things, and it was so long St. Louis. This place still felt less like home than like the place I'd escaped to. That would come with time. Starting anew seemed the solution, but it wasn't easy. No one here knew my past. I had no one here to talk to.

Long distance calls were no solution. I'd severed my St. Louis ties. That was part of starting over.

I told Stu a little about the dreams during a lull at work. I had to tell someone. "This is the same dream. It's more than recurring, it's like it is expanding."

Stu admitted it was wild and said he'd had a recurring nightmare as a kid. I reiterated that it was not simply recurring but expanding, "like a seed." Stu asked if I was sure they were all separate dreams.

I asked what he meant.

"Is it possible that part of the latest dream was just imagining that I'd dreamt parts of the dream before. The mind can do freaky shit sometimes."

I said no, but then began to doubt myself. Maybe all those disconnected pieces had somehow collected in my head. Vic was definitely a recurring element. Earlier in the week, I'd even masturbated thinking about him. In my mind the abandoned building was also the same, and the stoop, and the truck backing up... "No, I'm sure every dream was part of some larger dream that is being revealed, like I'm walking in and out of a looping movie."

Stu ruffled his my hair. "That's so crazy. Like a puzzle. Maybe thinking about the dream is what's making you dream about it. If these dreams are building into something, it's probably wise to start writing them down." He had a point. "That way you can get clear about what's going on. Seeing it in print might help you start to get a handle on it. You're a writer, maybe this is all part of the great American novel being revealed to you."

"I doubt the great American novel is going to contain graphic gay sex."

"You never know, my friend. The times they are a-changing."

So like Stu to reference Dylan. The dream journal was a wise suggestion. That afternoon I wrote down all I could remember from the dreams about Vic and the abandoned building and the room and the footsteps and the storm in a spiral notebook. I kept it, along with a pen, beside my bed.

I didn't have the dream that night, or the night after. Or even the night after that. Just when I began to think I'd been making too much of it, the dream returned.

As water dripped from the ceiling, I noticed the crack in the plaster was widening. Bits of ceiling plopped to the floor like spoonfuls of oatmeal. It was all falling apart. Larger pieces of plaster followed until I could see exposed boards. With decay happening above, I wondered if the same thing was happening below. At any moment the floor might buckle and give. I moved towards the door. The floor felt secure, but for how long. Lightning flashed. Thunder shook the walls. Plaster dust filled the air. As I opened the door, a large chunk of plaster landed with a thud on the bed. In the hallway the sound of the falling rain was deafening. Flooding was evident at the back of the building.

Staying near the wall, I made my way down the steps. At the landing, I rounded the corner to the front foyer. I heard a creaking, then a crash behind me. The stairway had separated from the wall and crumbled. Every part of the old structure was falling apart. Soon it would be rubble. Water streamed down the walls. Worried the supports holding the stone arch I was huddled below would give way, I stepped into the downpour. I sprinted across the street to the entryway of another building, but it offered little in the way of shelter. The door was a slab of metal. No knob. No latch.

I heard the flapping of what sounded like a giant bird. In the next flash of lightning, I saw the thrashing sleeve of a heavy tarp rolling in the wind. The blue shroud covered the skeleton of a new construction just up the block. That seemed my best option for shelter. I dashed from the entryway and down the street, ducking under the flapping tarp and into the shrouded building.

The rain was deafening on the tarp, like being inside a drum. The site smelled of fresh-cut lumber and was a maze of vertical support beams, door frames, and cross beams. It was mostly dry inside. The drumming of rain on plastic lessened as I moved into the heart of the building. The next flash revealed a silhouette some distance ahead. It was Vic. He'd taken shelter here as well. Vic lit a cigarette. He'd been waiting for me. The rain made his words unclear, but it sounded like he said, "I knew you'd come."

I was about to ask Vic what he was talking about when he brought a finger to his lips and said, "Trust me."

Headlights from a turning car revealed the building's frame, light and shadow racing over the tarp with the car's movement. When I turned back, Vic was beside me. "Got any more cash?" He was near enough to feel the warmth and pulse of his body. I smelled the cigarette on his breath.

When I reached into my front pocket, the money was there. Vic shoved the cash in his pants without counting it. "You'll always be paying for this."

Vic backed me against a support beam beside a stack of drywall and pinned my arms overhead. "Couldn't stay away could you? Couldn't resist a trip to the dark side." Vic ground his pelvis against me. "This is what you want, ain't it?" This felt different from our first encounter. Trade did not do this. "Yeah. You feel that? You want me to fuck you with that?" Before I could answer, Vic shoved his tongue down my throat.

Lighting cast a cage of shadows about us. Everything shook with the rumble of thunder. Rain or sweat made Vic's skin look unreal. His face glistened like a mask. I closed my eyes and tried to vanish into the moment. After more kissing, we dropped our pants. Vic spit on his hand and reached down to stroke himself. His eyes were black and flat, as though they were entirely composed of his pupils. I assumed it was a trick of the light.

Vic stroked me. I reciprocated with a sweaty grip. He was flush to his belly in a few strokes. His quick response turned me on. I wanted to work every inch of it with my mouth.

When I dropped to my knees, Vic caught me by the arm. He kissed my ear and growled for me to strip. "Slowly," he added. "Make me want it. I hear you like to put on shows."

I did as he asked. Getting out of my wet clothes felt good. I took extra care in rolling my underwear down slowly, working to show off my ass to its best advantage. I tossed my underwear at his feet.

Vic picked them up, took a whiff, and tossed them aside. He raised his white t-shirt over his head. The serpent tattoo was gone, but I was enjoying the view too much to care. In the next flash, I noticed Vic was covered with swirling patterns of black hair. I didn't recall that. Maybe the rain just made his body hair more apparent. When Vic bent to remove his shoes, I saw his ass was covered with thick down as well.

He shook the rain from his hair. "Now suck me," he finally said. Maybe he didn't even say it aloud. Maybe the command came from his stance and his expression. I was eager to comply. I inhaled the heavy musk of his junk before licking the length. Moments later he was face fucking me. I felt his cock swell and I felt the nuance of every vein. Vic pushed me away. I fell to the sawdust. Vic told me to get myself ready.

I'd been ready since I first saw him.

"You've had this coming for a while." Vic motioned towards the other side of the room. He said to bend over the saw horse. I did as I was told. The smell of freshly cut wood was overwhelming. I saw his shadow and turned to see him in the flesh. He looked different again. I didn't much care. A good fuck would make things right. I heard Vic move behind me. My grip tightened on the legs of the saw horse. I tried to will myself to relax.

I felt someone kissing on the side of my neck.

"Did you fall asleep?" asked the man beside me. I felt the stubble and realized I was in my own room. A bedside lamp cast shadows across my wall. Thunder rumbled outside.

There was a naked man in my bed who looked nothing like Vic. I must have jumped. "Who the hell are you?"

The man moved away on the bed. He held his hands out before him. "Are you kidding me?"

"No, who are you?"

"Are you fucking with me?"

"No, who the fuck are you?"

The man hopped from bed and reached for his clothes. "Settle down. We met at The Barracks and had a couple drinks. I'm Andrew, remember? You invited me over to mess around. Seriously, are you fucking with me? Were you on something?"

On the nightstand was a condom wrapper and my lube. "What did we do?" I could feel what we'd done, but I had to be sure.

By then Andrew was fully dressed. "We had sex, you know. Good sex if you ask me. Then you fell asleep for a minute."

I sat up in bed, rubbed my head, "It was raining and..."

Andrew shook his head. "You're scaring me. The storm just passed through. Do you need a glass of water or something? Are you okay?"

I lit a cigarette and kept quiet. I needed to wrap my head around this.

"It's starting to thunder again. Maybe that's what you heard. Maybe you were dreaming and got all mixed up with that. I think I'd better go and let you sleep off whatever you're on. I'll let myself out."

My voice was flat and distracted. "Yeah, sure. See you around."

Andrew left without another word.

I took a drag from my cigarette and began to recount the strange chain of events in my notebook. How could I forget picking up a trick? Someone must have drugged me at the Barracks. But I don't even remember going there. Last thing I knew I was going to bed. Could I have done all of that in my sleep?

Was I going nuts? I thought I was going to lose my mind last year, but I survived all that. St. Louis was behind me. Maybe this was a side effect of my medication. As I tried wrapping my mind around the latest mystery, I penciled a couple sketches of Vic. The first drawing was as he appeared in the first dream. The

169

second depicted him at the construction site. Neither drawing bore a passing resemblance to the trick I'd apparently met at the Barracks. I tossed the lube across the room and lit another cigarette. I was too afraid to go back to sleep.

I had to share what was happening with someone. The next day at work I told Stu.   "What?"

"I told you it was crazy."

"Whoa, you're sure this guy didn't just give you something."

"I don't think he did. And like I said, I have no memory of even going to the Barracks."

Stu rubbed a hand on the back of his neck. "That is some crazy shit."

"That's what I was afraid of."

"No, what's happening is crazy, not you. From the sound of it, this is some serious fourth dimension shit going on. It's more common than you think. A lot of unexplained things happen every day that no one hears about."

I should've known sharing the dream with Stu would spark one of his conspiracy/alien/multiple dimension theories. Stu was the only folk singer I knew who sang about the social problems of other galaxies. I poured myself an iced coffee and asked Stu if he had a theory.

"I have no fucking idea whatsoever, but something is definitely happening my friend."

Things had been going fine for me here until the dreams started. The move had been wise. I'd been getting on with life as best I could. My tendency for isolating was nothing new. Not healthy, but not new. I was still functioning.

The dreams brought all my imagined progress to a halt. No matter how busy I made myself, how much I exercised, or how much I drank... I couldn't shake the lingering fear that things had followed me here. The thought of seeing a new doctor and explaining everything filled me with dread. A doctor had the power to confirm my fears.

The dream went away for a while. I vowed to give it no more power. My mind was in control. These dreams would have no more power over me. None. I bought a sound machine and listened to ocean tides at night. That worked... for a few days anyway.

Rain pelted the tarp. Shadowed shapes could be seen. Bent over the saw horse, I didn't expect what was next. No pain of entry, but the gentle lap of a tongue. I felt myself relax. The sensations continued as the storm's roar blended with my moans. Vic knew what he was doing. Another line most trade never crossed.

A moment later I felt the weight of his hands on my shoulders. In the lightning's flash, I saw the ring. A double silver band. I had one just like it. Had I given him my ring along with the cash?

All thought scattered with the first thrust and gradually reassembled as I began to relax and pain became pleasure. Vic's ring dug into a boney part of my clavicle. His hands were different now. Not only his touch, but the texture of the hands themselves. They were manicured. Softer. Vic whispered "Still don't remember? Trust me." The thrusts assumed a rhythmic flow as Vic's moans began to blend with my own.

Vic's hands moved to grip my nipples and twist. So practiced. So familiar. Hustlers knew all the hot spots. I felt the come start to rise inside Vic as well as in myself. So close. I imagined a roller coaster car climbing

171

higher. Seeing over the top of the rise, and knowing the thrill and rush of what was to come.

I heard a laugh. Familiar. Not Vic. Now was not the time. Just a bit more and we'd be over the top and consumed by the explosion. In another moment, it arrived. I screamed into the blackness and awoke to the sound of the ocean waves.

I was clutching my pillow and crying. The name on my lips was not Vic.

I rolled onto my back. Those hands. That ring. The laugh. All so familiar. Unmistakable. This dream wasn't an unfolding, it was a reveal. This dream was a return.

In the bathroom was a small box I kept near the sink. Cufflinks. A couple of chains. And the double-banded ring I'd seen in the dream. I thought that was all in the past. I thought I'd left the best and worst of my life behind in St. Louis. But it had returned.

I remember the day I received that ring. Hank had bought us identical bands for our anniversary. The double-banded rings were a symbol that we'd always be together. We'd sworn on it. By then we'd been lovers for two years and had lived together for one. Hank was as long term as I'd been with anyone. There were no taboos between us except dishonesty. We'd shared sexual fantasies and tried to make them happen, from bondage to role play. As an actor, Hank was big on the latter with a thespian's love of exhibitionism. Monogamy didn't feel like a prison. With Hank, it was more like a playground.

On our second anniversary, I planned something special. We went out for a nice Japanese dinner. Over two scoops of mint ice cream, I told Hank I was taking him to a bathhouse. Despite his being sexually adventurous, Hank had never been to one, yet he'd always wanted to go. When he saw I was serious, he brushed back an overhanging curl of black hair. He was eager, but also anxious.

"Trust me," was all I said.

We walked four blocks to the bathhouse that warm October night. No reason to take a cab. The full moon was haloed by a haze. Hank agreed that it was something to behold. We shared a kiss. The wind was starting to pick up. A woman covered in rags shouted something in a vacant lot in the next block. We looked at each other and quickened our pace.

The attendant said no rooms would be available for at least an hour. We took lockers for the time being. After checking in, we stripped down and hung our clothes in adjoining lockers. Beside us, several guys dawdled to admire the view. Hank was an olive-skinned Greek. Dark. Hairy. Great smile. His high, rounded ass was supreme. I am lean with fair skin, red hair, and blue eyes.

We walked the labyrinthine corridors. The scent of disinfectant and musk, the rose-tinged lighting, and the thump thump thump of the music resurrected memories for me. Before Hank, I'd clocked miles walking these well-worn halls. I'd fucked and been fucked and assorted other things under this roof. I learned safe sex here. The layout differed slightly, but not much. I even recognized some of the faces and a few of the bodies.

I loved seeing Hank take it all in. He was torn between keeping up with me and lingering to look in open doors with men reclined on cots. Stroking themselves. Beckoning eyes. Sometimes calling out. Some knelt with asses high, waiting. For some the need had become primal. The specifics didn't matter. Only want. Only now.

We passed a maze of glory holes and cubicles before entering the TV room. A porn loop was playing, a fresh load was dripping from the actor's chin in the color-faded film. Hank eyed the men lounging semi-nude and nude on the carpeted risers and platforms around the room. Some of the men were giving us both the once over. Some tried to be secretive. Others were blatant. Hank moved closer to me.

I said "trust me" a second time before leading him to a carpeted dais in the middle of the room. Pulling him close, I grabbed his ass through the towel and began deep kissing him. Hank loved being on stage, loved an audience, loved to kiss, and loved having his ass played with. The combination was likely to dispel any second thoughts he might be having.

In the flickering light of the porno, I took my hands from Hank's butt and ran them over his muscled chest. A moment later, I planted kisses across his furry stomach, tonguing his navel. Reaching beneath Hank's towel, I stroked his cock. Before he could protest, I yanked the towel from his waist, threw it to the carpet, and took his cock in my mouth.

The crowd shifted. Hank dropped his hand to my head, winding his fingers in my hair. His eyes were closed. He was muttering something softly in Greek. I didn't need a translator to get the gist of what Hank was saying.

Some of the men in the TV lounge moved closer. Others, who were making the rounds, paused to watch. If they wanted a fuck show, who were we to disappoint. We were much better than the video. Some reached out

174

to test the boundaries. I knocked their hands away. This wasn't audience participation.

Guys began to stroke themselves beneath their towels. Some did it outright. As we continued, more towels fell to the floor or were flung over shoulders. A half-circle had formed. Watching us. Watching each other. Wordlessly masturbating. The sound of stroking was a potent aphrodisiac. A chorus of desire.

I bent Hank over and licked the backside of his low-hanging ball sack before kissing the hairy globes of that exceptional ass. I said to get on all fours. In no time my tongue was lapping his hole.

The energy of the men around us was making Hank more responsive. He was playing to the crowd, spreading his ass cheeks, arching his back, grinding his butt against my tongue. My index finger slid inside him. I tore open a condom pack with my teeth and rolled on the sheath. I rubbed it along the furry length of Hank's crack before positioning myself at the muscled ring.

I eased inside. There was a sigh from the circle of voyeurs. The audience had doubled. Some of those gathered began to fondle and suck each other. Hank was lost in the sensations, but aware of a rapt audience. He reached down and stroked himself. He leaned back and kissed me hard. I tasted the ginger from dinner on his tongue. I tried to maintain control, but the scene fueled my lust. Watching the men close in for a better view took me to the edge. I smelled their sweat, felt their labored breathe on my back and shoulders, and heard whispers of encouragement. Their lust enveloped and propelled us. They were no longer silent.

"Yeah, fuck that ass."

"Give it to him."

"Go deep, stud. You like putting on a show?"

175

A hand squeezed my ass and brushed across its surface, I was too lost in the moment to push it away. Another reached up for my nipples. I moaned. I'm hard-wired that way. Another stroked the back of my thighs. My balls. Every nerve in my body was afire. I curled over Hank and whispered, "Look at the desire in their eyes." Hank moaned. Actors always get off on a responsive audience.

A moment later, I pulled out and yanked off the condom. I'd seen enough porn to know that an audience appreciates a good money shot. By then my cock was flush to my belly. A lube-coated hand reached over and gripped my shaft. Those strokes were too good to resist. In a few seconds, I exploded. The hand continued, eventually smearing the residue across his lips. I closed my eyes and licked those fingers clean. When I opened my eyes, the stranger had already disappeared into the crowd.

Hank leaned into me. I ran my hands over his hirsute chest. His nipples were hard beneath my fingertips. Hank was fucking his fist with abandon. "That's it. Do it, baby. Everyone's wants to see it. Come on, give 'em what they're waiting for." His body shook. Muscles twitched. He was there. The crowd closed in for moment and seemed to pause before exhaling as one.

Curtain.

The show was over.

The crowd dispersed.

In the porn loop, the blonde surfer, wet suit around his ankles, was kissing down a lifeguard's muscled belly.

Hank's back was dewy with sweat. His hair was damp. The room reeked of jizz and stale poppers. In the flickering light of the film, I fingered Hank's curly black hair. I always knew it was love with Hank because the aftermath was as good as the sex. Even here, sex brought out a tenderness that I'd only read about in books or seen in movies. I kissed the nape of Hank's neck, "Happy anniversary, baby."

The attendant on the PA system announced our locker numbers. We were to report to the front desk. A room had become available. We'd gotten our money's worth, but we decided to stay a while longer. After all, it was our anniversary.

We moved to small cubicle of a room. I told Hank I needed a rest before another round. We spooned on the thin mattress in the reddish light of our small room with the chicken wire ceiling. We locked hands. I looked at our double-banded rings and kissed Hank's hand. That was the last thing I remembered.

When I awoke, Hank was gone. My head pounded from the red light and thumping music. I assumed Hank was prowling on his own. I knew how curious he could be and this was a carnal wonderland. The surreal light. The pulsing music. Dozens of eager and willing men.

I didn't begrudge Hank's exploring, but it did complicate things. He didn't have a room key. I opened the door and lay back down. A couple guys came in and played a bit. Nothing developed. After a while, I went to look for Hank. As an exhibitionist who also liked to watch, his potential for adventure here was endless. I searched all three floors, but didn't find Hank. Maybe he was in someone's room, or a booth, or we'd just missed one another. In another hour, I checked at the front desk. Hank had checked out two hours ago. The attendant said he was alone. Had something had happened? Maybe he'd had a panic attack or rush of guilt over being there. Why would he leave without saying anything?

I assumed he went home. Checked out and took a cab to our place. But he wasn't there either. Maybe he had stopped somewhere for a nightcap. I couldn't imagine Hank would've hooked up with someone at the bathhouse and left.

The following day, I filed a missing persons report. The police were not sympathetic or cooperative. Disappeared from a bathhouse? They assumed it was a lover's quarrel or a tryst or a drug thing or the remorse of an unfaithful partner. The next day I got a call from the station. They found someone who fit Hank's description. The detective asked me to come down to the station. There were photos.

His beaten body was found at a construction site several blocks from the bathhouse. There was no sign of sexual activity. His wallet was missing. The police asked if anything else was missing. I asked about a watch or a ring. Both were gone. Apparently Hank was the victim of a mugging and/or hate crime. I could still see the headlines, the grainy photo of Hank and another of the crime scene.

I couldn't sleep. My doctor gave me an open prescription for something. I started taking it around the clock. I'd been taking it ever since.

The weekend after Hank's murder, I walked by the construction site where his body had been found. The industrial part of town was quiet on Sundays. A blue tarp flapped in the wind behind the yellow CRIME SCENE: DO NOT CROSS tape. I sat on a stone stoop across the street and stared at the place where Hank had died.

If I hadn't taken Hank to the bathhouse none of this would have happened. If only we had left instead of getting the room. If I only would have stayed awake. If I only I knew why Hank had left. I had so many questions and so many regrets. Moving on was impossible when so much remained a mystery. All the unknowing made our time together seem like a dream. The ring on my finger was proof that the past two years had been real.

Hank's family arrived and removed all his things from our apartment. They took the body "back home" for the wake and burial. They asked if I wanted to attend.

"People didn't know. We don't want to complicate things."

I became his friend.

I was guilty enough to comply.

There were storms on the day of his funeral. I can still hear the sound of the downpour on the tarp beside the grave. I stared at my hands and twisted my ring as Hank's family wept.

His parents were polite, but I was a reminder of a part of Hank they never acknowledged. I suspect they blamed his "lifestyle choice" for his tragic end. They thanked me for being such a good friend to their son and paid for my plane ticket back to St. Louis. They said to keep in touch, but didn't mean it. I was a symbol of the chapter in Hank's life they were eager to forget. I took a cab to the airport.

Our apartment was suddenly too large and too vacant. His presence was everywhere. I thought about getting a roommate or a smaller place, but decided to leave town all together.

I doubled my medication and vowed to put this behind me. I'd make a fresh start. I'd run from my past before. Physical distance can be a great remedy. Five years earlier, I'd left my hometown in Virginia to come out of the closet and be myself. Now the country boy I'd once been was all but gone. I could shed this identity as well. A new place would allow me to be a single gay man instead of a gay widower. I would will myself to change.

That week I gave notice, broke my lease, and made plans to move. We had very few friends, and those we had stepped aside. No one argued. No one said I was being rash. No one wanted to get involved. The situation was messy. Having me leave was a relief. I was a grim reminder of something best forgotten. Packing was easy. Most of the things in the apartment were Hank's, and his family had almost picked it clean. The rest I gave away or priced to go at an apartment sale. Aside from some photos and knick-knacks, the only reminder I have of us was the ring.

I found a place quickly. The following week, I found a job at the Bean Factory. I liked the fast-pace and mostly mindless work. A solid combination for forgetting. The effects of trauma and self-sedation did the rest. I made friends with Stu almost immediately.

He knew I moved here after a relationship. That's all. Lies came when I began to talk about my ex and how we argued. Initially, I said it to make Stu feel better when he talked about the problems with his girlfriend. But the fib expanded and became something else entirely. Creating a myth was another way to forget. I shared all sorts of untruths. Hank became Brian, and Brian and I fought and made threats and cheated. Brian had spray painted something on my car. Brian made me leave town. "His insanity scared me." Stu was happy things with his girlfriend weren't that crazy.

I thought Hank was gone forever. Then the dreams began. I remembered Hank's distinctive laugh, and the ring on that familiar hand clamped on my shoulder. The swirling black hair across a torso. Those things were him. Memory residue. I wondered how Vic became part of the story. There was no one like him in my past. He had nothing to do with the crime or my memories of Hank that I could recall.

Hank's murderer was apprehended the week after his body was discovered. By the time of his arrest, he'd already pawned the ring. The thug confessed, was convicted, and sentenced. He hadn't meant to kill Hank. I remembered him in the courtroom. He was cuffed and downcast and quietly wept throughout the trial. Seeing him like that made nothing better.

I'd once shared a fantasy with Hank about servicing rough trade. The fantasy came after passing a hot guy on the street with a serpent tattoo that wrapped around his torso. I'd seen the man for no more than a moment.

"You like?" Hank had said.

I nodded.

Hank asked where my fantasy with that guy would take place.

"Somewhere desolate, an abandoned hotel." I said that I wanted it to be dirty and anonymous.

I remembered more fantasies we'd shared.

I mentioned sex in an old hotel, Hank had a fantasy about fucking at a construction site. I'd forgotten. As the mist surrounding my memory lifted, I recalled other things. Lying awake and talking about being together forever. That brought such assuredness and security. I remembered our fingers lacing and a pact that we'd never be apart. I thought all that was shattered and the fragments lost behind the DO NOT CROSS tape of a crime scene. I slipped the ring on my finger.

Hank once said, if worst came to worst, he'd visit me in my dreams. He kissed my hand when he said it. I remembered the look in his eyes when he said it and wondered if Hank had returned, wrapped in the fantasies we once shared. A moment later I stopped wondering. I knew it was true.

Hank had revealed himself slowly, through the fantasy, then with his laugh, and finally with the ring. I sat upon my bed, gobsmacked by what it all meant. He'd come back. His partial return only revealed the extent of what I'd lost. I cried more than I had since losing him.

That night, my dream came without disguise or mystery. I dreamt of the first time we'd had sex. Our second date. We went back to Hank's apartment after dinner at a Mexican restaurant. We knew what was coming. We sat on Hank's back porch and talked. Smoked a joint. We were stoned and smiling. During a lull in conversation, I gave his crotch a squeeze. Hank smiled and wrapped a hand around the back my neck, pulling me closer. We kissed.

A moment later, we were grinding on the creaking porch. Our hands exploring each other. I fingered Hank's fly and felt the hardness beneath the denim. I fumbled to release it. A moment later, I broke the kiss and went down on him. Hank muttered something in Greek and soon we were 69ing on his back porch.

Afterwards we both lay back on the porch and sighed in unison, which made us laugh. We felt the first drops of rain and heard a creaking on the porch above. That night we went another round in his bed. Nothing hurried in this round of lovemaking. Eventually, we lay in each other's arms and watched the summer storm.

In my dream, the memory expanded. As we spooned and watched the storm, Hank kissed my shoulder. He said there was no need for guilt or remorse. He'd always love me. As I watched the lightning, Hank said he'd left the bathhouse that night because he was nauseous and needed fresh air. He'd dressed quickly, checked out, and stepped outside. He planned on calling but couldn't get reception on his cell. One bar. He walked a little further. Two bars. That was all he remembered before the darkness, and then the light.

Hank kissed me and said he'd always be with me. He kissed me a second time, "Always."

I awoke smiling. Hank had been visiting me all along. We'd made a promise. Always was unconditional.

I never again feared the night. My dream became our dream. We'd be together forever on an eternal playground of carnal pleasure. No rules. No limitations. And no end. A promise was a promise.

Owen Keehnen

Writer and historian Owen Keehnen is the author of several fiction as well as non-fiction books. His fiction, essays, columns, and interviews have appeared in dozens of magazines and anthologies worldwide. He currently does LGBTQ content for the Chicago tourism website and magazine, Choose Chicago. Keehnen is the co-founder and senior biographer of the LGBT organization, The Legacy Project (LegacyProjectChicago.org) which celebrates the contributions of LGBT people in history. He was inducted into the Chicago Gay and Lesbian Hall of Fame in 2011 and currently lives in Chicago with his husband, Carl, and their two dogs, Flannery and Fitzgerald.

By Owen Keehnen

Night Visitors

Love Underground

The Matinee Idol

Young Digby Swank

Vernita Gray: From Woodstock to the White House

The LGBT Book Of Days

Gay Press, Gay Power – contributor

The Sand Bar

We're Here, We're Queer

Jim Flint: The Boy From Peoria

Leatherman: The Legend of Chuck Renslow

Doorway Unto Darkness

Nothing Personal: Chronicles of Chicago's LGBTQ
Community 1977-1997 - co-editor

Rising Starz

Ultimate Starz

Out and Proud in Chicago - contributor

More Starz

Starz